HAWK

IRON ROGUES MC

FIONA DAVENPORT

HAWK

Callum "Hawk" Maughan handled security for the Iron Rogues with brutal efficiency. Whether it was protecting their bar, their businesses, or their secrets...he kept the club's world locked down tight. Until Gemma Moffitt needed help and unraveled everything.

Gemma made her living behind the camera lens. A boudoir photographer with strict rules and even stricter privacy, she thought she was safe until someone hacked her server. Desperate, Gemma turned to the Iron Rogues for help and found much more than she bargained for. Hawk wouldn't just protect what was his. He'd destroy for it.

1

GEMMA

"That's the last one." I lifted the camera from my face and let it hang from the strap around my neck. "You did amazing."

Ellen let out a breath that was half laugh, half relieved exhale. "Thank goodness. That was terrifying."

I flashed her an encouraging smile. "Yet you did it anyway, which is pretty much the definition of being brave."

"Yay me," she murmured with a soft chuckle, clutching the sheet tighter around her chest. Her cheeks were flushed, and her legs were tucked beneath her as she leaned against the back of my velvet chaise. "I don't think I've been this anxious since the day I got married."

Snagging a robe from the hook on the wall, I crossed the room toward her. "A different kind of nerves, though, right?"

"Yeah, this time no one's expecting anything of me but me." She gripped the sheet in one hand while taking the robe from me with the other. "It's not like I sent invitations to my boudoir photo shoot like I did with my wedding. I don't even plan to show them to anyone else."

I turned around to give her privacy while she stood and slipped into it. "You never know. Once you see how gorgeous you are in these photos, you might want to plaster them everywhere."

"You're sweet, but I don't see that happening." When I turned back, Ellen was cinching the belt at her waist, her expression and body language more at ease than it had been when she first walked in. "Thanks for making me feel...not ridiculous, I guess is the best way to put it."

"I'm glad you didn't feel ridiculous because it's the last thing I'd call you." I lifted my camera again, cradling it in both hands like the extension of myself it had become. "Brave and beautiful are definitely more fitting."

She blinked rapidly, the corners of her mouth turning up. "I almost canceled this morning. I kept looking at myself in the mirror and wondering what I was thinking when I decided to do this. I'm thirty-six, recently divorced, and I haven't worn anything remotely sexy in a year. It just felt like pretending, even if only for myself."

"I see a lot from behind my camera lens. Please trust me when I say you weren't pretending. You were reclaiming yourself." Her gaze flicked to mine. "That's what boudoir is about for most of my clients, even the ones who originally book the session because they want photos for their partner. At their heart, my photo shoots aren't for someone else, just women remembering they're allowed to feel sexy for themselves."

"How did you get so smart?" She shook her head with a laugh. "I'm old enough to be your mom, but here you are, schooling me on something I should've realized on my own."

I rolled my eyes. "Only if you were a teen mom."

"Okay then, big sister."

"That's more like it." I winked before walking her through the upload process, pointing out how the files I would share with her were encrypted. Then I handed her a card that had a password printed on it. "I'll send a secure link to your private gallery tomorrow. You'll have full control—download, delete, whatever you want. No one else will ever see these photos unless you choose to share them. This password will get you in, and the link will expire in two weeks. If you need longer than that, just let me know. They'll be numbered, so you can just tell me which ones you want me to fully edit and print for your package."

She clutched the collar of the robe, pulling it tighter across her chest. "Thanks. I appreciate how careful you are with them."

I headed into the front of the studio so she could get dressed. When she joined me, I helped her gather her things, offered her a bottle of water from the mini fridge, and double-checked that she had everything.

At the door, Ellen paused and looked back at me. "This meant more than I can say. I feel as though maybe I can look at myself without flinching now. Like I undid some of the damage my ex did to my self-esteem."

My heart squeezed. "That's exactly what I hoped for."

She reached for the door handle. "You're really talented, Gemma. And not just with the camera."

"Thank you." I tucked a piece of hair behind my ear. "Drive safe, okay?"

"I will."

The door clicked shut behind her, and I stood there for a second, letting the stillness settle. The space always felt different after a session. Warmer, somehow. Especially with clients like Ellen who'd come to me hoping to reclaim some of their femininity. They were the reason I started doing boudoir shoots in the first place. And why I never wanted to stop.

I left the music playing at a low volume, just enough to keep the silence from feeling too loud, and moved around the studio for my usual post-session routine. I powered down the lights, unplugged the softbox, and coiled the cords with practiced hands. Replaced the lens cap. Folded the white sheet Ellen had used and added it to the laundry basket.

Then I moved to my desk and slotted the memory card into my editing laptop. A secure connection dialog popped up immediately, and I entered the password without hesitation. The photos began to transfer, thumbnail by thumbnail, and I opened the encrypted drive to prepare the backup.

I gave the file transfer a few more seconds, then clicked over to check my to-do list for the day. I still had a couple of emails to send and a small stack of receipts I hadn't entered yet.

I leaned back, stretched my arms overhead, and let my gaze drift toward the back corner where my little kitchenette was tucked against the wall. I wasn't ready for dinner yet, but I was hungry.

I grabbed a granola bar from the drawer and perched on the arm of the loveseat while I unwrapped it.

While I chewed, I opened my favorite images of Ellen and did some light edits. Just some cropping, a little exposure tweak here and there before I uploaded them to the file-sharing service I used that allowed for end-to-end encryption.

Ellen hadn't believed me when I told her how beautiful she looked, but I hoped that would change tomorrow when she looked at the full gallery. Something about seeing yourself through someone else's lens when the lighting was soft made it click in a completely different way.

Once I checked off the last of my tasks, I shut everything down and walked back to the little house I'd bought with some of the money from my parents' life insurance. I'd been so excited to find one with an unattached garage that I was able to convert into my studio.

I spent the rest of the afternoon and evening working on Ellen's photos, then sent confirmation texts for my appointments for the next few days. Spring was always a busy time, and while the back-to-back appointments could be brutal, I adored my job so it always seemed to fly by.

But I made sure to take a day off every week if only to get paperwork and business stuff out of the way. I'd spent this morning editing and was checking over my to-do list while the completed photos were added to the client's private gallery.

I reached for my phone out of habit but noticed the red notification badge sitting on my email app. Tapping it open, I didn't think twice about checking the message even though I didn't recognize the sender. As a small business, I received seemingly random emails all the time, and sometimes I ended up with a new client because of them.

The subject was a little odd, though.

Thought you'd want to know...

The message loaded slowly, and my breath caught in my throat when I saw the image embedded in the body of the email.

It was a photo of Ellen. Topless and wrapped in the white sheet from her shoot, her smile soft and a little uncertain. It was one of the final frames I'd taken and the first that I had uploaded to the drive only she and I had the password to.

It had been cropped tighter than my original. Whoever sent the message had adjusted the aspect ratio, zooming in on her face and chest.

There was only one line of text below the image.

She should've kept her clothes on.

The phone shook in my hand as my fingers clenched around it, and for a split second, I forgot how to breathe.

I didn't understand what I was seeing. Nobody should have been able to access that photo.

My stomach knotted so hard it felt like I'd been punched.

Nothing like this had ever happened before.

I backed out of the email and tapped frantically into my file manager, checking the encryption log and verifying the folder integrity. Everything looked normal to my untrained eye.

But right before I shut the screen, I glanced at the download history and gasped. The files had no history of being accessed by anyone but me and the client, but there were dozens of folders with downloads made on the same day, yet there was no log-on recorded.

Something had obviously gone horribly wrong because that photo had obviously been stolen. And sent to me. Which made it likely that it was the same person who had taken copies of all the other photos as well.

I couldn't run the risk that the women who'd trusted me with an intimate piece of themselves were about to be violated in the worst possible way. I needed help, and there was only one person I could think of who might have the connections I needed to get to the bottom of this quietly.

Someone I trusted.

My heart pounded as I opened my contacts and scrolled to Lainie Evanson's name. We hadn't talked much since she left for college, but she was the kind of friend who wouldn't hesitate to help no matter how long it had been.

Pressing the phone to my ear with trembling fingers, I whispered, "Please pick up. I don't know who else to call."

2

HAWK

My trigger finger twitched, but it wasn't because I was itching to shoot the man with my gun pressed against his forehead. Not that the guy cowering in front of me didn't deserve it, but because my phone was vibrating for the third damn time in my back pocket. I smirked, and the pathetic drug dealer flinched when he noticed my expression shift. I let the muzzle of my Glock drift just slightly off center, dragging it along his temple as I pulled the phone out with my free hand.

The screen lit up with a number I knew well.

Midnight.

My boss and co-owner of Iron Shield. Our motorcycle club, the Iron Rogues, owned the other half.

It was the direct line to his office.

The man didn't waste time or words, and he knew exactly where I was and what I was doing. If he was calling me mid-interrogation, it wasn't to shoot the breeze.

And answering wasn't a suggestion.

"Reaper," I muttered, stepping back and tilting my head toward the bastard we were threatening. "It's Midnight. If he even breathes wrong, shoot him somewhere painful. But don't kill him. Yet."

We'd caught the asshole trying to push product through the club's bar, The Midnight Rebel, where I often helped out with security when not on assignment for Iron Shield.

When it came to Iron Rogues territory, we didn't fuck around. We practically owned the entire town of Old Bridge, Tennessee, along with most of the surrounding area. What wasn't technically ours still fell under our protection. Nobody took a breath without us knowing about it. That included law enforcement and local politicians.

The Iron Rogues weren't some fictional MC ripped from a movie script. We operated outside the law, but we lived by a strict code. Honor. Loyalty. Brotherhood. And our own brand of justice. When it came to people who fucked with the club, we were the judge, jury, and when the situation warranted it, the executioner.

We had zero tolerance for drugs in or anywhere around the club.

That alone was reason enough to have a conversation with the bastard currently about to piss himself in front of us. But it wasn't just that. We'd uncovered a plan to boost a shipment of priceless cargo acquired through questionable means. We were escorting the delivery for our best client. Nic wasn't just our prez's best friend—he also happened to be the head of the DeLuca Crime Family.

This idiot clearly had no idea who he was mixed up with. No sane person would ever rip off one of our organizations, much less two.

Now we expected the sniveling prick to cough up the details. He hadn't been all that cooperative so far, but judging by the whimpering, it wouldn't be long before he cracked.

With one last dark look, I stalked over to the corner of the room and pressed the phone to my ear. "Yeah?"

"Back to the office," Midnight said, voice gravel-thick and unbothered. "Now."

"You're pulling me off this?" I started this job and intended to finish it. "He's almost cracked—"

"Reaper will handle that shit. Get your ass back here now."

My spine stiffened, and I wanted to argue, but then he added, "You've got a new assignment. Priority."

Priority. I could practically hear the air quotes.

Shit.

I should have known. Midnight never redirected my work unless it was serious.

"Be there in twenty," I ground out before hanging up.

I stalked out of the small concrete building we called The Room, hidden deep in the woods behind the compound. The place existed for exactly this purpose—secluded, silent, and soundproof.

I stopped by the clubhouse and took the time to scrub off the flecks of blood and change into clean clothes before I hopped on my bike and headed to Iron Shield HQ.

When I arrived, our receptionist was typing away at her desk.

"Midnight's waiting," Sheridan muttered, not bothering to look up when I passed.

"Nice to see you, too, baby sister," I grumbled, mouth quirking up.

She finally glanced at me, pushing her red glasses up her nose before glaring daggers at me.

I paused long enough to flash her a lopsided grin. "Still pissed?"

"You lied to my date and told him I was underage," Sheridan spat.

"You're not old enough to drink." I pointed out with a frown.

"That's not what he thought you meant, and you know it!"

"He was too old for you."

"Maybe if I was actually sixteen!"

"You're nineteen. Close enough."

"He was twenty-two."

"He was a dick." I shrugged and sauntered toward the stairs that led up to the building's second floor.

"Twenty-two is not too old for me!" she shouted.

"Too dumb is worse than too old."

Her glare tracked me until I headed up the stairs. I grinned to myself because she'd get over it. Eventually.

I took them two at a time and swung into Midnight's office. He sat behind his desk, flipping through one of the matte-black folders we used for client files. His expression was unreadable, his dark eyes scanning details like they were code waiting to be cracked.

"Stop pissing off the front desk," he said without looking up.

"Where's the fun in that?"

He finally looked at me and scowled. "Don't give a fuck if you're having fun, Hawk. If she quits because she gets sick of dealing with your shit, you'll be the one sitting at that desk. Unless you're dead."

Nothing in his expression suggested he was joking. But I decided not to dwell on that.

"Won't happen," I assured him. "She loves working for me."

"She doesn't work for *you*, asshole. She works for *me*," Midnight growled as he leaned back in the chair, fire burning in his eyes so briefly I wasn't sure I'd really seen it.

"Close enough." I dropped into the chair across from him, my muscles loose but my senses sharpened. "What's the job?"

He slid the black folder across the desk. "Protection detail."

My brows pulled together in irritation. "You pulled me off a critical interrogation for glorified babysitting?"

Midnight's expression held a dark warning, and I

pressed my lips together to avoid saying anything else.

As an enforcer for the club, I outranked him, but just barely. Here, though, he was my superior, and I respected the chain of authority. Plus, Midnight didn't put up with shit from anyone. Only Fox and Maverick—our prez and VP—knew his background. Or anything that wasn't surface-deep. To the rest of us, he was a mystery. All we knew was that he'd worked in security of some sort. He was cold, calculated, and deadly as fuck.

His tone was even and low. "If I put you on trash duty, then that's what you'll do, Hawk."

I nodded.

"Besides, it's not babysitting when it involves family. She's Lainie's friend."

That shut me up. Lainie was the younger sister of our treasurer, Phoenix. And the best friend of Savage's old lady, Tamara.

I'd take a bullet for Lainie. No questions asked. Same way I would for Tamara or any of the other women my brothers had claimed as their own. They were protected. Cherished. Nonnegotiable.

If this friend meant something to Lainie, I'd do it. But I wasn't happy.

"This is more than bodyguard duty," Midnight

continued. He gestured to the client file. "Gemma Moffitt. Boudoir photographer. Women-only. Keeps her work encrypted and locked down, but someone cracked her system. Stole files."

I opened the folder and flipped past the summary page.

The first image hit me like a fucking sucker punch.

A small, square ID photo in the top corner. Warm brown eyes. Heart-shaped face. Cute, pert little nose. And full, soft lips made for sin.

A thick toffee-colored braid draped over her shoulder, drawing my eyes to voluptuous tits that had my cock turning hard.

Her features had a natural softness, but something sharp was behind her gaze. A spark. Confidence and warmth wrapped in curves that made my blood go hot.

What the fuck?

I swallowed hard and flipped to the next page. There were copies of the stolen images. I studied them with an almost clinical eye. They were tastefully done—soft lighting, silhouettes, implied nudity. I looked for commonalities among them, a possible clue as to why these particular photos were chosen.

Then I reached the last one, and I felt like someone had clocked me in the solar plexus.

It was her.

Holy fucking shit.

Her head was thrown back, facing away from the camera. But I didn't need her face to be visible to recognize that body.

My cock hardened instantly, my libido reacting like it had been waiting for this exact moment to come alive again.

I hadn't felt this in years. Not a flicker of interest. Not even a twitch. The guys assumed it was because I hadn't gotten over my ex, but they couldn't be more wrong. I'd realized years ago that she wasn't meant for me.

I'd been young and dumb back when we got engaged. Hell, it hadn't even been my idea. Our moms had basically planned the whole thing. If we hadn't had the longest engagement in the history of my hometown, I probably would've been miserably married to her now.

My years-long dry spell wasn't me pining for her. I just hadn't been drawn enough to a woman to put any effort in. But Gemma made my mouth water and my cock throb painfully.

My hands curled into fists as I stared at the

photo. She was draped across a vintage couch wrapped in a loose white silk robe that barely clung to her shoulders. The tie was cinched just enough to draw attention to her narrow waist and wide, round hips. One leg was bent, and the robe parted just enough to show miles of smooth skin all the way to the edge of her lace panties.

Holy hell.

Her tits strained against a matching bra, the robe slipping down just enough to expose more creamy skin. The cups of the lingerie were so low I could almost see the dark area around her nipples.

I flipped back to the first page and looked at the face that I knew, without a doubt, belonged to the body in that last picture.

And I lost my fucking mind.

"Who's seen this?" I snarled.

Midnight blinked once, calm as ever. "Just Deviant and me," he said, referring to our resident tech genius. "Though I doubt Deviant really looked at them when he pulled the portfolio together."

"It better fucking stay that way." My tone low and dangerous. A warning.

I already wanted to crack his head open and scrub the image from his mind. The thought of anyone else seeing Gemma like that caused my possessive feelings to turn murderous. When I found the son of a bitch who'd stolen that photo, he was gonna wish he'd never been born.

Midnight's expression tightened, and his voice was low and steady when he said, "I'm going to let you explain that before I fire your ass."

I didn't want to fill him in. At that moment, neither Midnight nor Deviant knew there were photos of Gemma in the file, and I wasn't happy with the idea of pointing it out. But Midnight didn't make idle threats.

"The last photo. It's the photographer." My jaw clenched hard as I forced myself to admit I was feeling territorial over a woman I'd never even fucking met. "I don't want anyone else seeing her like that."

Midnight's brows lifted, and something flickered in his eyes. "Maybe you're not—"

"Mine," I growled before I could stop myself.

Silence fell between us. I realized I was on my feet, knuckles white around the folder.

Finally, I cleared my throat and tried to level out my voice so I appeared calmer than I felt. "I'm taking this job."

He studied me for a long beat. Something was working behind his dark eyes, and I prepared myself to face his wrath if he tried to hand Gemma over to someone else. It wasn't gonna happen.

I had no idea why I was so determined to keep this case. Or why the fuck my body was on fire over a fucking picture. It made me feel like my mind and body weren't my own. And that pissed me off. I was never, *never* out of control.

Eventually, he leaned back and gave a slow nod. "Alright. You meet her tomorrow. Lainie will bring her to The Midnight Rebel in the morning since you're upgrading Savage's security feed."

I didn't answer. Didn't have to. Just turned and walked out.

A glance at my watch told me I was late for my shift at The Midnight Rebel.

Dammit. I was not in the fucking mood to grit my teeth through drunk assholes, slap away a few wandering hands, and pretend not to hear every groupie giggling over which biker they wanted to "accidentally" fall into.

But Savage was taking the night off, and I'd promised to fill in as extra security since Fridays were always chaos.

The walk to the bar only took a few minutes, but I spent it trying—and failing—to get my shit together.

I wouldn't let this bombshell interfere with my life. For fuck's sake. I didn't even know the woman.

I wasn't like my other brothers, who were already locked down and happily pussy-whipped. I'd stayed detached. Focused. Professional.

I'd never even looked twice at the women who hung around the bar. But now I couldn't stop picturing Gemma on that couch. The image was burned into my brain.

When I got to the bar, the doors banged open as I stormed in.

"Late," Savage muttered, glancing up from the prep work he was doing before the bar opened, and he bailed with his wife and kid.

"Take it up with Midnight," I grunted as I marched toward the bar. "New assignment."

I snatched a glass and a bottle of my favorite whiskey, poured two fingers, and tossed it back.

"Fucking client briefing," I muttered. "What kind of a name is Gemma, anyway?"

Gorgeous.

That was what it fucking was.

Just like her.

Shit!

"Sounds soft. Too soft," I muttered as I took the glass and whiskey with me into the kitchen. I poured a third drink and downed it slower this time. "Probably sweet. Probably fragile."

But that wasn't what had me on edge.

She was dangerous in a way I couldn't explain.

And somehow, she already belonged to me.

Gemma Moffitt had no idea what she'd done to me. Or what I was going to do to the bastard who stole her photos.

But she was about to find out.

3
———
GEMMA

I paced back and forth across the hardwood floor
in my living room, practically wearing a track
through the wax while I waited for Lainie to arrive.
My nerves were probably frayed more than they
needed to be since she'd assured me that her brother's club could help, but I couldn't stop freaking out.
Too much was on the line.

It wasn't my reputation as a photographer that I
was worried about. My expenses were low enough
that I could survive for a long time on the rest of the
money my parents had left me if my business failed.
But my clients wouldn't emotionally recover so easily
from their privacy being invaded...and neither
would I.

The midmorning sun streamed through my

curtains, but I still felt like I stood in shadow. The tension in my chest hadn't eased since I received the email last night. Every time I blinked, that photo of Ellen flashed behind my eyes. The thought of showing it, and all the other stolen pictures, to a stranger made my stomach twist, even though I had a good reason for doing so.

A sharp knock on the door made me jump. I wiped my palms down the front of my jeans and forced myself to take a breath before opening it.

Lainie stood on the other side with a soft smile and two travel cups of coffee in her hands. Her hair was pulled back into a ponytail, and she looked effortlessly put together in leggings and a leather jacket that somehow didn't clash with the sparkly pink polish on her nails.

"Hey," she said, holding out the coffee like a peace offering. "You ready?"

"Depends how loose your definition of 'ready' is," I replied, stepping aside to let her in.

She gave me a once-over as she entered. "You look great."

"Thanks." I took one of the coffees and sipped it gratefully. "I really appreciate you driving all this way. With finals coming up, two hours is a lot. I would've understood if you couldn't make it."

She waved off my gratitude. "Eh, it'll be good for me to get some baby cuddles in with Baxter. Maybe I'll get lucky, and Lindsay will pop a little early. Then I'll already be here for my niece to meet Auntie Lainie right when she's born."

I rolled my eyes with a snort. "Don't let your brother hear you say that."

"Yeah, he loves me, but he would not be cool with me hoping my sister-in-law goes into early labor," she agreed.

I had seen how protective Phoenix was of his wife and son when they brought Baxter in for photos. The vibe of that shoot had been the opposite of my boudoir ones, but it had been a blast.

"I guess we should probably get going."

She flashed me a soft smile. "Good call. I don't know him that well, but Hawk doesn't strike me as the most patient guy. But he specializes in this kind of thing, so you'll be in good hands."

I hesitated, the coffee suddenly heavy in my hand. "So this guy...he works for the Iron Rogues?"

Lainie nodded. "He's one of Beck's club brothers, but he technically works for Iron Shield. It's the security company that's partly owned by the club."

"Sounds like he's the perfect person to help me,

like you said," I muttered as I followed her outside to her car.

She laughed. "Yeah, none of the Iron Rogues are exactly sunshine and rainbows. But Beck told me that Hawk doesn't mess around when it comes to security stuff."

"Great." I rubbed my fingers along the seam of the coffee cup. "Perfect. Just the kind of person I want to show my boudoir shots to."

"I hate to break it to you, but with how these guys work, he's probably seen them already." Lainie's expression softened at my horrified expression. "But you don't have to tell him that any of the photos are of you unless you want to."

"I know," I whispered. "But I will. If it helps stop whoever's doing this, I'll do whatever it takes."

That wasn't a decision I'd made lightly. But I wasn't about to back down now.

Lainie nodded once, like she understood what was going on inside my head. "Alright then. Let's go see Hawk."

I tried to settle my nerves as Lainie pulled into the lot in front of The Midnight Rebel—a bar owned by the Iron Rogues.

I'd driven past the bar more times than I could count, but I'd never been inside. Even if I'd had a fake ID claiming I was twenty-one, I wouldn't have dared try it here. Not at a place owned by the Iron Rogues. That would be asking for more trouble than I needed.

Rows of motorcycles lined the front like a warning. Chrome glinted in the sunlight, and I couldn't look away.

I swallowed hard as Lainie parked and killed the engine.

"You good?" she asked, glancing over at me.

"Ask me again after I meet Hawk." I smoothed my hands over my jeans. "I need to keep my game face on so he doesn't think I'm this weak girl who's about to fall apart."

She reached over to grab my hand. "You're the furthest thing from weak, Gem. You didn't stick your head in the sand and hope this problem would go away. Now you're about to walk into a biker bar to talk to a stranger who has most likely seen you practically naked. Even if he doesn't know it's you. All so he can help you track down the bastard who took them. That's badass."

I let out a shaky breath. "Thanks. That helps. Sort of."

"Come on."

Lainie unbuckled and got out of the car, and I

followed a few steps behind, reminding myself to keep breathing. She opened the door and gestured for me to walk into the bar. I stopped just inside to look around, feeling her come up behind me. The low lighting and dark wood made the space feel intimate and a little dangerous. Leather booths lined one of the walls, with wood tables and chairs scattered throughout the open space. The bar was wide and polished, and I heard the soft clink of glass as someone organized bottles on the shelves behind it.

She grasped my elbow to lead me toward the wall of booths. A few of the men scattered around the room looked up as we passed. They were massive. Tattooed. Dangerous. And all of them wore a leather vest that announced to the world that they were an Iron Rogue.

I scanned the room, searching for someone who looked like they might be expecting us.

Then I locked eyes with one of the men at the bar, and everything else faded away.

He stood tall and proud. Like he owned the place.

He was at least six-foot-two and built like a battering ram in a black T-shirt that clung to a chest thick with muscle and arms that looked as though they could easily snap a man in half. His forearms flexed, the veins roping beneath tanned skin in a way I had no business noticing but couldn't stop staring at.

His sleeves were pushed up past his elbows, and his black hair was slightly tousled. Scruff shadowed his jaw, and his brown eyes were locked on me.

They were calm when I first saw him, but the instant our gazes locked, that calm seemed to crack. Something flared behind them. A kind of fire I didn't understand but felt all the way down to my bones.

I'd never felt the instant punch of attraction before, but there was no doubt I was experiencing it now. My breath caught, and I had to blink to break the spell he was weaving around me with just one look.

It didn't do much good, though.

He didn't smile. Didn't nod. Didn't look away. Just watched me, still as stone.

It was more than enough to make a lasting impression...and that was before he walked over.

4

HAWK

The second she walked through the door, I knew.

It wasn't the kind of knowledge that eased in slowly. It hit like a punch to the sternum. Sudden, sharp, and deep. Unlike anything I had ever felt before. My world narrowed to a single point—*her*.

Gemma.

Her long, toffee-colored hair gleamed under the soft amber lighting of the bar. Those soft brown eyes framed by thick lashes were big enough to swallow you whole. Her cute little nose crinkled as she looked around, visibly unsure if she belonged here. And her sinful lips were made to fucking wreck a man. They parted on a breath I swear I felt in my bones.

She had full tits, a narrow waist, and wide hips made for gripping. For holding down. For breeding.

The tight jeans she wore clung to hips made to ride. My bike. My hands. My mouth. Her snug dark blue sweater did nothing to hide the curves that could so easily bring a man to his knees.

And I'd seen her in lace.

Fuck! My cock stirred, hard and heavy, thick in my jeans.

I'd memorized every curve from the photo in her file. It had been tattooed into my skull ever since Midnight handed me the dossier. But seeing her now —real, flushed, shifting slightly behind Lainie like she wasn't used to this kind of attention—*nothing* compared to the real thing. She wasn't just hot...she was everything. Feminine and fierce, soft and lethal. And almost a foot shorter than me, which only made me want to wrap her in my arms and shield her from the world.

My cock throbbed even harder against my zipper, the metal teeth digging into the sensitive skin. I clenched my jaw and forced myself to breathe through the pain. Every inch of me screamed to move, to take, to claim.

But I stayed rooted to the floor. I couldn't make a

move yet. Not when she was looking at me for help. She needed protection, not possession.

Not yet.

Fox, Maverick, and Deviant were posted near me at the bar, watching. I didn't need to look to know their eyes were on her too.

"Easy." Deviant snorted into his drink. "You look about five seconds from dragging her into a dark corner and making her forget her own name."

Maverick's voice cut in. "Might want to save the caveman routine for when she's screaming it, yeah? Right now, you just look like a guy about to lose his shit."

Fox chuckled, arms crossed as he leaned against the brick column near the end of the bar. "Judging by that look on your face, I'm guessing the photo didn't do her justice."

My body went still, and I felt almost feral.

He hadn't seen it, I knew that. Fox was also completely obsessed with his old lady and in no way a threat to my claim on Gemma. But logic didn't do a damn thing to the animal in me that roared at another man even mentioning her like that.

"Don't," I bit out, low and sharp.

Fox raised a brow, cool as ever. "Relax, brother. It was just an observation."

I stepped in close enough to make the warning hit. "Observe someone else."

A beat passed. A flicker of amusement crossed his face—just enough to needle me—but he didn't push. Probably because he sensed that I was a second away from snapping necks and torching the world.

"She walked in, and your jaw damn near hit the floor," Deviant muttered with a crooked grin. "Pretty sure your dick saluted before your brain caught up."

My jaw flexed. His would be the first neck I snapped. He was already on thin ice with me, knowing that he'd gotten even a small glance at Gemma's photo. "Keep running your mouth and see what happens, asshole."

They all laughed, but there wasn't a hint of mockery in it. Just the kind of shit only brothers who'd already been hit with their own freight trains of obsession could give.

Fox's smirk was cold. "Relax, brother. We get it. But you've got eyes like a loaded weapon. Just don't forget where the safety is."

I finally looked away from her and met his stare head-on. "There is no safety."

Then I turned my focus back to my woman.

Lainie stepped in behind Gemma, guiding her

toward the booths lining the far wall. Her voice was low and reassuring, but Gemma remained alert. Cautious. Her eyes scanned the room while her hands twisted around the strap of her bag.

She stopped when her gaze found me. Her lips parted, and her eyes widened just slightly—like her brain and body had registered me before she could talk herself out of whatever she felt. *Good.* Because she was going to belong to me. She just didn't know it yet.

Maverick moved to stand, but I lifted a hand, signaling them to hold back.

"Let her breathe," I murmured.

Deviant gave a knowing smirk, already in on what I hadn't said out loud. Fox raised an eyebrow but stayed put.

I rounded the bar slowly, keeping my movements loose and casual. I wasn't about to scare her. She already looked like her heart was in her throat. But it wasn't just from nerves. There was heat in those eyes, too. She was trying to mask her reaction and bury it under all that tension in her shoulders, but I saw it. Her breath hitched, and I caught the flash of burning desire in her gaze before she blinked it away.

She felt the pull just as much as I did.

I stopped in front of her and let my eyes roam

down her body one more time—slow, deliberate, possessive—before meeting her gaze again.

"Gemma." My voice was low and steady, letting her hear the calm even while my blood pounded in my ears.

She swallowed hard, then nodded. "You must be Hawk."

Her voice was soft and sweet. But there was steel underneath it. Even my name sounded different coming from her mouth. Softer. Curious.

"Let's grab a booth," I said, jerking my chin toward the far corner.

Gemma's eyes widened, and Lainie glanced over my shoulder, smirking just as I felt the presence of my brothers as they walked up beside me.

"We'll meet you over there," Lainie murmured, leading Gemma away.

My girl followed her friend, her movements smooth but a little stiff. She didn't seem to be used to the attention. Or maybe she was just trying to figure out how to carry herself in front of a bunch of dangerous bastards like us.

"I got this," I grunted.

Fox raised an eyebrow but said nothing. Deviant, of course, didn't let the opportunity pass.

"Sure you don't want backup?" he said with a

teasing drawl. "Looks dangerous. All five-foot-two of her."

"She doesn't need the lot of us hovering," I muttered. "Just hang back."

"Whatever you say," Maverick murmured, but there was a smirk tugging at the corner of his mouth.

Gemma slid into the booth with Lainie at her side, and I took the seat opposite, my thighs brushing the edge of the table as I settled in, hands flat against the wood to keep them from twitching toward her. I could still feel the phantom weight of that dossier in my hands. The photo was seared into my mind. But with her in front of me now, the picture was so much more vivid.

She was temptation wrapped in vulnerability. Confidence barely caged under the weight of whatever danger she'd walked into.

Up close, her scent filled the air—warm and clean with an underlying hint of something floral. My hands curled on the table. I wanted that scent to surround me, to be on my skin and soaked into my sheets.

Focus, asshole.

"Start from the beginning," I said, my voice low and even. "Know some of it already, but I want to hear it from you."

Gemma hesitated. Her fingers fidgeted with the sleeve of her shirt before she stilled them with a breath. "Someone hacked into my archive."

"Encrypted?" I asked, though I already knew.

She nodded. "It wasn't supposed to be possible. I paid for a custom system. It was built by someone who came highly recommended."

Lainie scoffed. "Yeah, well, they clearly weren't Iron Rogues recommended. You're ours now, Gem. We've got Deviant."

Gemma gave a shaky smile and turned to me. "She's right. I just...didn't know where else to go. I'm scared. And not just for me. One of the images that was stolen was of a client. A very private one. And she's...she's really fragile right now. I can't stand the idea of her being crushed by this. The message in the email..." She paused, and I caught the way her throat worked as she swallowed, glancing at Lainie like she needed a second of courage before looking back at me.

"It said, 'She should've kept her clothes on.'"

I forced myself not to react. Not to let the rage boiling in my gut show on my face. She didn't need that kind of intensity right now. But my hands curled tighter against the table, the grain pressing into my palms as I clenched my jaw so hard I could feel it throb. Her voice didn't shake. She wasn't sobbing. Her hands trembled just slightly. Not from fear. From fury.

She was brave. Protective of her clients. And I fucking *loved* that.

But she was also watching me, wide-eyed and uncertain. I saw the question lingering there—*Can I trust you with all of this?*

I softened my voice. "You're safe now. But you gotta tell me everything if we're going to protect you."

I didn't rush her. I just met her gaze and let her feel my calm and certainty.

Her shoulders loosened the tiniest bit, and her lips parted. She stared at me for a long second, like she was trying to figure out why she already trusted me. I wanted to tell her she didn't need to understand. That some things didn't make sense on paper. They were just meant to be.

After taking a deep breath, she nodded. "There's one more thing."

I already knew what she was about to say, and my pulse pounded, roaring in my ears.

"There's a photo of me," she whispered. "In the stolen files. One I never meant for anyone to see."

My hands clenched on the edge of the table.

Hard. Wood bit into my palms. I kept my voice even, careful not to let the fury slip into my expression. "You sure?"

"Yes," she whispered.

I *knew* it. From the second I saw that curve of hip, that dip of collarbone. My gut had gone tight, my cock harder than steel.

But she didn't need my carnal reaction right now. She needed calm. Control.

"I'm setting up surveillance at your place and studio." I redirected the conversation before I did something stupid. Like drag her over the table and kiss the fuck outta her in front of everyone. "Deviant's already working on tracking the files. I'll meet you at your house in a few hours to go over security."

A small smile curled up the corners of her lips. "Okay."

I didn't want to let Gemma go. Every protective instinct in my body screamed to keep her within reach. But I had no excuse to make her stay. Yet.

Lainie nudged her. "Come on, Gem. Let's go."

Gemma paused, her warm brown eyes meeting mine. "Thank you, Hawk."

"Callum."

Her brow rose.

"My name is Callum."

"Okay. Um, thank you, Callum."

I nearly growled. I wanted her to say my name the same way again. Soft and breathless. Like it was a secret.

But instead, Lainie muttered, "Just to be clear, that's two of my close friends now claimed by the club. I really should start charging a matchmaking fee."

Gemma blinked, blushing furiously, but I didn't miss the way she peeked up at me from under her lashes. "What?"

"Never mind," Lainie huffed as she slid out of the booth first, tugging Gemma along with her.

Gemma looked over her shoulder as they headed for the door. There was confusion lurking in those brown pools. She didn't understand her reaction to me.

I forced myself to keep my feet planted where they were. There was plenty of time to educate her later. After this shit was handled.

When the door shut behind them, I finally let myself breathe.

"She's gonna wreck you," Fox said from behind me, sounding amused as hell.

Deviant made a low whistling sound as he

dropped into a chair and kicked his boots up on the table. "Heard your balls hit the floor the second she walked in."

"Shut the fuck up," I growled.

"Big, bad Hawk. All that brooding and cold silence," Deviant chuckled. "And now you're walking around with a hard-on and puppy eyes."

I clenched my hands into fists so I wouldn't strangle him. "You must really want to bleed today."

Ignoring my warning, he grinned and quipped, "I give it a week before he's moved her into his room and turned into one of those 'can't function without her' types."

My voice was threaded with steel, and my stare was deadly. "Keep testing me, Deviant. See how that ends."

Fox smirked. "Two days. Tops."

"Fuck both of you."

That just made them laugh harder.

Maverick snorted. "Guess it's your turn to go soft. Don't worry, happens to the best of us."

"Not me," I muttered.

Liar.

"Right," he deadpanned, calling me on my bullshit. "You're just vibrating with bloodlust because you *care so much about justice.*"

I flipped them all off and stalked toward the back hall, already counting the minutes until I could see her again.

Planning how I was gonna make her mine.

And when I found the bastard who'd dared to touch her work, steal her photo, and make her live in fear...he was going to learn exactly what it felt like to be hunted by a man with nothing to lose when it came to the woman he'd just claimed.

5

GEMMA

I checked the mirror again. For the third time. Okay...the fifth.

I wasn't even wearing anything fancy. Just the same tight pair of jeans that did amazing things for my butt and a cropped sweater in a shade of soft gray that matched my mood. I'd changed shirts twice already before settling on this one. It was comfortable and didn't scream that I was trying too hard but still looked good on me. Maybe Callum would just assume I'd gotten cold and changed for that reason. April in Tennessee was known for having unpredictable weather.

I'd put my nervous energy to good use in the few hours since Lainie had dropped me off at my house so she could go visit her brother. My house was probably cleaner than it had ever been. I wiped down the kitchen counter again even though it didn't need it, then adjusted a framed photo on the wall. It was one of the many nature shots I'd taken before I got into boudoir.

My house wasn't much. Two bedrooms, one bath. But it was mine, and Callum was about to see it for the first time.

I wanted my home to make a good impression on him, and I'd done all that I could by the time he knocked on the door.

I wiped my hands on my jeans—a nervous habit I needed to break around him—and tried not to look like I was about to pass out as I crossed to the door. But when I opened it, all my carefully rehearsed calm evaporated.

He was taller than I remembered. And bigger, somehow. Maybe it was because he was dressed in all black, from his fitted T-shirt that clung to thick biceps to his dark jeans that hugged his thighs like a second skin.

That dark scruff still shadowed his jaw, and I wondered if he had to shave twice a day to keep it at bay.

The stray thought flew out of my head when his dark brown eyes locked onto mine.

Heat bloomed low in my belly, but it was the other feeling he sparked that rattled me more. Safety.

I barely knew Callum, but he made me feel like nothing could touch me as long as he stood there. And that scared me almost as much as the messed-up situation he was helping me with.

"Hey," I managed, my voice too breathy for my liking.

He gave a short nod. "Gemma."

"Come in." I stepped back, hoping he couldn't tell how nervous I was.

He moved past me with the grace of a stalking panther, his gaze sweeping the entryway and living room, lingering longest on the windows.

"You don't have to do a full tactical sweep," I joked, trying to break the tension. "I swear the plants haven't turned against me yet."

He didn't even smile. "Where's your breaker box?"

I blinked. "Um, in the garage. Which is my studio space now."

He nodded once. "We'll head out there after I do that tactical sweep, which is very much necessary."

Pausing by the window, he tapped the trim. "No sensor. I'll add magnetic contacts here and here. Glass break detectors, too."

I blinked. "You're planning to install stuff yourself?"

He glanced over his shoulder at me. "Absolutely."

Butterflies swirled in my belly as he moved on, muttering about sightlines, exterior exposure, and interference shielding. I trailed him but did not understand at least half of what he said.

When we walked to the kitchen, he scanned the back door and the small window above the sink. "Deadbolt's decent. I'll upgrade the strike plate. Add a motion sensor on the exterior light. And a silent alarm pad behind the pantry door that only you and I will know about."

My eyes kept getting wider. "Is this the part where you tell me I should sleep with a knife under my pillow?"

"No," he said without missing a beat. "Because I'm installing a panic button near your bed."

I stopped in the middle of the room. "Wait, what?"

Callum finally turned to face me, arms crossed over his broad chest, his expression carved from stone. "You said someone accessed your encrypted system and sent you a threat. That makes this a targeted breach, not a random hack."

"I know," I whispered.

"I take targeted threats seriously."

"Okay, but..." I gestured vaguely around us. "Don't you think this is a little over the top?"

"Not even close."

His voice held no hesitation. No room for argument. He wasn't doing this halfway.

My pulse fluttered in my throat as I realized this might not just be a job for him.

He didn't have to be this thorough. He didn't have to walk through my house like he was cataloging every weakness, every vulnerability. He didn't have to install sensors himself or rig panic buttons.

But he was doing it anyway. For me.

No. I mentally shook my head, scattering that train of thought. *For Lainie.*

But even though that was the most likely reason, I couldn't help but hope he felt the pull between us as strongly as I did.

"Need to check out the studio and that breaker box."

I hadn't realized how tightly wound I was until we left the house. We stepped out into the sunlight, and I immediately felt like I could breathe again. The air was cool and crisp, and the narrow path between the house and garage gave me something to focus on besides the towering man walking beside me.

My heart was still racing from the panic button comment. From his eyes. And from the way he hadn't even blinked when I'd asked if this was too much.

"I converted the garage as soon as I moved in," I said, just to fill the silence. "It was kind of a mess when I bought the place, but I knew right away that I could turn it into a real studio."

Callum nodded once but didn't say anything. Still, I couldn't seem to stop.

"I got into photography after my parents died." The words came out softly. "I needed something to help me make sense of everything. That let me escape for a while."

His gaze flicked toward me at that, his expression sharp and unreadable.

"I started with nature stuff. Landscapes, plants, things that didn't move too much. Then I did a headshot for a friend, and I realized I was kind of good at it. People opened up for me. They trusted me. And that mattered more than I expected."

The gravel crunched under our feet as we reached the studio door. I paused before unlocking it, fingers hovering over the key.

"I think that's why I started doing boudoir. Women would come in nervous and unsure, and they'd leave with their heads held high like they remembered something about themselves that they'd forgotten. Most of the time, it isn't about being sexy for someone else. It's about claiming that power for themselves."

I glanced over, bracing for the awkward expression I usually got whenever I tried to explain my motivation behind boudoir photography. Most people assumed these types of photos were all about sex, but that was very rarely the true purpose. However, the only reaction I got from Callum was a softening of his dark eyes.

"I bet you're even better than you think at that," he said finally, his voice low. "Helping people feel seen."

His approval meant more than I expected, surprising me as I pushed open the studio door and stepped inside.

Soft natural light filtered through sheer curtains I'd pinned just right to catch the glow, and the familiar hush settled around me.

This space was somehow even more mine than the house because it was where my creativity blossomed.

No one had been in here since I discovered the breach. Not even me. I hadn't let myself come back until today. But with Callum behind me, I didn't feel afraid.

He didn't say anything as he entered, but his gaze moved slowly over everything. The backdrops, chaise, and table where I kept props and fabrics folded neatly in labeled bins. I wondered what he'd think when he spotted the ornate bed with the iron posts on the wall across the room. But his attention didn't feel judgmental. Just focused.

And the silence didn't bother me anymore because I realized that Callum was a quiet man.

But every time his eyes came back to me, my breath caught.

The way he watched me reminded me of how I studied a client before I began taking photos. It was as though he was memorizing every detail. Every line of my body, even fully clothed. Every move I made.

I turned away before I climbed him like a tree. "I'll make sure the studio's clear tomorrow when you start installing the security stuff."

He didn't respond right away, and I wasn't sure he'd even heard me until he said, "Lock up tight tonight. I'll be here at eight."

I walked him around the side of the house, heart already thudding again with each step.

He paused in my driveway, his dark eyes holding mine for one long, impossible moment. Then he nodded and walked away.

I watched until he reached his bike, forcing myself to turn away from the sheer sexiness of him throwing one long leg over the seat. But it didn't stop me from thinking about how much I wanted him to stay.

6

HAWK

The moment I pulled my truck into her driveway the following morning, I knew I was walking into enemy territory—because nothing about this place belonged to me yet. She wasn't even mine yet—as far as she knew—but I already felt more for Gemma than I ever had with any other woman. She was already in my blood, and I was determined to own a piece of every part of her life. The house wasn't flashy, just a small cottage, but it fit her perfectly. Pale blue siding, white trim, and big front windows with gauzy curtains that fluttered behind the glass. Tucked behind it was a converted garage that looked like it had been rebuilt practically from the studs up when she converted it into a studio.

From the outside, the place projected a sweet,

quiet life, and my need to protect Gemma strengthened.

I texted her when I parked, and as I approached the front door, she cracked it open just wide enough to let me in. Then she aimed a soft smile at me, causing an unfamiliar warmth to spread in my chest.

"Morning," I said gruffly, my eyes devouring her and reminding me how fucked I was. Tight jeans hugged those incredible curves, a soft purple T-shirt stretched across her tits, and that long toffee hair was in a ponytail hanging down her back.

Damn.

She wasn't just sexy as fuck. She was beautiful. Real. And already under my skin.

"Good morning. Come in." She swept her hand out toward the cozy living room. "Do whatever you need. I'll be out in my studio so I'm not in your way."

"Could never be in my way, baby," I replied as I stepped inside.

She blushed hard, and I was tempted to slide a finger over the soft skin of her cheek, but I shoved my hands into my pockets instead.

"Um. Well. I have work to do anyway. Just, um, come out to the studio when you've finished with the house."

I nodded and curved my lips into a half smile.

Her eyes dropped to my mouth for a moment, and her cheeks turned an even deeper shade of red. It was fucking adorable, which wasn't a word I ever expected to use.

She spun around and swiftly walked across the room toward the kitchen that was part of the open concept design. After grabbing a stack of papers off the counter, she tossed one last look at me before slipping out of the back door.

Once she was gone, I stepped farther inside, and my senses were overwhelmed.

Gemma was everywhere.

The air smelled soft and clean, but with that same trace of something floral clinging to the edges. Sweet, warm, and feminine.

Her throw blanket was crumpled on the couch like she'd just gotten up, and a half-read book lay on the cushion beside it with a pencil stuck between the pages. On the end table was an empty glass with a wooden coaster beneath it. And a pair of slippers were kicked halfway beneath the coffee table.

It wasn't messy. Just lived-in.

I could easily picture my things mixed with hers, and my chest tightened. This didn't feel like just her home.

It *was* hers.

But now I wanted it to be mine.

Correction...*ours*.

Until I was here to protect her, I would make sure she was as safe as possible. I'd mapped out the entire security overhaul before I even got here. Spent half the night going over specs and redundancies. Silent alarms and glass break detectors on the doors and windows. Motion sensors in the front and back-yard, especially around the studio. Wireless cameras with full-circle coverage, infrared, and cloud uploads. It was a fortress in progress.

I started with the perimeter, working fast and quiet. Installing the outdoor sensors, testing signal strength, and camouflaging the devices so no one would spot them unless they knew exactly what to look for. Then I headed back inside to set up the base system.

That was when the all-business wall I'd built around me cracked.

Her bedroom door was half open, and I tried to ignore it. Tried like hell. But it didn't fucking work.

I stepped into the room, quiet as a ghost, and paused just inside the threshold. Her bed was made with an embroidered white quilt and decorative pillows. They had frilly edges, and I cringed imagining what my brothers would say if they saw how girly it was and knew it was where I slept.

Well, the single ones anyway. Since I knew I'd be willing to deal with all that feminine shit if it meant being with my woman, I assumed the guys with old ladies felt the same.

Something on the shiny, hardwood floor caught my eye. It was halfway under the bed skirt, like it had been accidentally kicked there and gone unnoticed.

My breath got stuck in my chest when I realized what it was.

A pair of panties.

I swallowed hard.

They were light blue and made of lace.

All the blood in my body flowed straight to my groin.

The strings at the side would easily give way with one sharp tug.

Fuck!

I bent down slowly and picked them up, running the delicate fabric between my fingers before bringing them to my face. Burying my nose in the spot that covered her pussy, I inhaled deeply. My cock turned rock hard, pressing against my zipper like it wanted to rip free.

The lingerie carried the scent of her skin, and my tongue tingled in anticipation of tasting her. I wanted to know if her flavor matched her natural fragrance.

Growling low under my breath, I stuffed the panties in my back pocket and headed for the bathroom to get my head on straight.

Only that didn't help because one of those circular birth control packs sat on the counter. It hadn't been there yesterday when she showed me around.

Oh, hell to the fucking no. My face twisted into a scowl as I snatched the container and popped the lid open with my thumb. All twenty-eight pills were still there. Not a single fucking one missing.

The breath I hadn't realized I'd been holding whooshed out. *Good.*

Because if I had it my way, she'd never take another one.

I took the whole damn thing and shoved it into my pocket with the panties. Then I slid a couple of her bottles of girly shit to the edge of the counter so it looked like some of it had been knocked over. A small trash can sat just beside the cabinet, so hopefully, she'd assume the pills had fallen into it.

I probably should have felt a little guilty at the

deception, but I had no regrets. There was nothing I wouldn't do to get what I wanted.

My cut on her back. My ring on her finger. My baby in her belly.

It wasn't a question of *if*. Only *when*.

I was finishing up the last of the interior cameras —one above the front door and another angled across the kitchen—when my phone vibrated.

It was Deviant, so I answered on the second ring, keeping my voice low. "Find anything?"

There was a pause before he spoke, which never meant anything good.

"Ellen's missing. Reported by her sister late last night. No signs of struggle. Phone's off. No activity on her accounts in the past forty-eight hours."

My chest went ice cold.

"Fuck," I muttered. "I have to tell Gemma."

"Yeah. And I need to talk to her. Everything she remembers about Ellen. Stuff they talked about, routines, whatever. Hopefully, she'll have information that'll help me piece together a timeline while you handle ground security. In the meantime, I'm digging into her life over the past week to see if I can find a digital trail to follow."

"Thanks," I grunted. Then I ended the call and shoved the phone back into my pocket. After gathering up everything I needed for the studio's security, I left the house through the back door and followed the path to Gemma.

When I walked inside, her back was turned to me as she adjusted the lighting. The place looked like something out of a dream. A classy but very dirty dream.

A plush chaise, strategically placed mirrors, a table covered with props, and...*shit*.

My eyes landed on the fancy bed on the far wall that I'd avoided thinking about when I noticed it yesterday.

I couldn't peel my gaze away from it today. Soft sheets were tangled up on the mattress, perfectly messy in a way that suggested they had been staged. Soft lighting bathed the bed in a hazy warmth that heated my blood.

And there she was, barefoot, her hair piled on top of her head and her clothes hugging every delicious curve. She was reaching up to fix a bulb, and her shirt lifted, exposing a smooth strip of skin above the waistband of her jeans.

My cock was instantly hard again, although it had never fully deflated, knowing her panties were in my pocket. The earlier temptations came roaring back with a vengeance, and I lowered the box in my arms to cover the enormous bulge in my leather pants.

"Fucking hell," I whispered before I could stop myself.

Gemma turned when she heard me, a question in her eyes.

But I couldn't speak. My gaze was drawn to the bed again, as if it had a magnetic pull and my jaw clenched.

"You okay?" she asked softly.

My eyes flicked to hers. She was watching me carefully, cheeks pink and her lips slightly parted.

All I could do was nod, my mouth too dry to speak.

"It's a prop," she said, brushing her ponytail over her shoulder. "The bed, I mean. For shoots."

I still didn't answer. Just nodded again. Because I couldn't trust myself to speak. Not without sounding like a fucking animal.

Then my phone buzzed again, breaking the spell so I didn't do anything stupid like rip her clothes off and shove my face between her legs.

I glanced at the screen.

DEVIANT

Need to talk to her. Today.

I was frustrated at the reminder of the news I had to break to Gemma, but I still replied.

ME

Okay.

Then I slid my phone back into place. Wishing like hell that I didn't have to wipe away her smile, I scrubbed my hands over my face. Then I dropped them to my sides and got it over with. "Ellen's missing," I said quietly.

Gemma's entire body stilled. "What?"

"She hasn't been seen in two days, and her phone's off. Deviant's trying to find a digital trail but wants to meet with you. See if you can remember anything that might help."

Her eyes filled with horror, and her hands pressed to her stomach like she needed to physically hold herself together. "Oh no. No, no. She's so sweet. And kind. Who would...why?"

"I don't know, but I'll find out." I stepped forward to pull her into my embrace. She came willingly, burying her face against my chest like it was her safest place.

And it *was*.

There was nowhere that Gemma belonged more

than in my arms. I held her tighter than I meant to. But she didn't protest or try to break away. My hands splayed across her lower back, fingertips brushing the top of her jeans.

She felt so fucking *right*. Fitting perfectly against me. Another confirmation that she was made to be mine.

My woman. Old Lady. Wife.

I wanted to hold her like this every fucking day for the rest of my life.

Eventually, she pulled back with a shaky breath.

"I should—I need to work," she whispered. "I need to keep busy and try not to spiral."

I didn't want to let her go, but I did. Barely.

She stepped away and moved toward her computer, swiping at her cheeks with the sleeve of her shirt.

At first, I searched for something to say, then I realized that the silence between us wasn't strained by tension. It was comfortable and easy. Like simply being in each other's company was all we needed.

I adjusted the bulge in my jeans and went to work setting up the final security feeds in the studio. I used the same method I would for any high-level asset.

Except this wasn't any client. This was Gemma. And that made what I found next a hell of a lot worse.

Buried in a light fixture above the chaise lounge, so small I nearly missed it, was a bug.

The device wasn't high-tech, but it was expensive enough to have decent audio. I looked closer. And video.

Fuck!

My entire body went still, then tight with fury.

They'd been listening to her.

Fucking *watching* her.

For who the fuck knew how long.

My jaw locked, and I turned to stare at Gemma's silhouette as she sat at her desk in the corner, the light catching her profile.

They'd been spying on her.

On *my* woman.

My pulse turned to thunder.

It didn't matter that she'd only been mine for a day. Or that she didn't even know it yet. This motherfucker was gonna suffer. No one fucked with the people I cared about. Especially not the woman who belonged to me.

After taking a picture and sending it to Deviant,

I snapped the bug in two, crushing the pieces in my fist as I marched across the room.

Gemma turned, startled. "What's wrong?"

"You're not staying here."

She stood, blinking in confusion. "What?"

"You're moving to the Iron Rogues compound. Tonight." My voice was hard, leaving no doubt that I wouldn't budge on this.

Her head cocked to the side, and her brows drew together. "Wait. What? No. I have clients. A business. I can't just—"

"You can," I snarled. "And you will. End of discussion."

Her lips parted like she wanted to argue more, but something in my expression made her close them again.

The last thing I wanted to do was make Gemma scared to be in a place that was usually her sanctuary. But she deserved to know why I was putting my foot down about this.

"The studio was bugged, baby. For the moment, you're not safe here."

Gemma gasped and covered her mouth with one hand as her brown eyes filled with tears.

I hated that I'd put that look on her face, so I softened my voice when I spoke again.

"You can work, but I'll be with you." I held up my hand when she opened her mouth to interrupt. "Not inside the studio. I'll be just outside. Watching. Because not one motherfucker is gonna come near you unless I say so."

She hesitated and glanced around with a defeated expression. Then she nodded slowly. "Okay. And I'll reschedule what I can."

I inclined my head in appreciation for her meeting me halfway.

"But I won't let this bastard derail my whole life," she snapped.

"He won't," I said, my voice dark. "Won't live long enough for that."

Her eyes grew wide, but she didn't comment on my threat. Instead, her shoulders drooped, and she gave me a soft smile. "I know you're only doing this because of Lainie, but I'm really grateful for your help."

My head popped up, and I growled, "Not doing it for Lainie."

Gemma hesitated, her expression puzzled. "Then...why?"

I prowled toward her, slow and deliberate. Backing her up until she hit the wall.

Then I braced one hand beside her head and the other on her round hip. Our eyes locked, and for the first time, I didn't mask the raw hunger, the primal need I felt for her. "I protect what's mine."

Her breath caught, her skin flushed, and her irresistible lips parted.

My control shattered, and I kissed her.

Hard. Possessive. A fucking claiming.

Her body melted against mine, and I deepened the kiss, letting her feel just a fraction of the heat burning inside me. My hands glided over her hips, down to her thighs, lifting her off her feet. I braced her back against the wall and ground my steel shaft against her hot center. She arched into me with a whimper, her fingers gripping my shirt as though she was afraid I might disappear.

I wasn't going any-fucking-where. However, this wasn't the right time to give in to our passion. Cursing a blue streak in my head, I pulled back just enough to let her slide along my body as I set her back on her feet.

Closing my eyes, I pressed my forehead to hers, trying to calm my racing heart. Her panting breaths rubbed her big tits against my chest, and I groaned in acute frustration.

When I could speak again, I grunted. "Pack your shit, baby."

"Why?" she whispered, dazed.

"Because if we stay here another minute, I'm gonna throw you on that bed and fuck you so hard the cameras will melt."

7

GEMMA

I didn't think I could feel more violated after my archive was hacked. But I'd been wrong.

The moment Callum told me about the bug he found in my studio, it felt as though the floor had dropped out from under me. This wasn't just a digital breach. Someone had come into my space so they could watch and listen at their leisure.

The studio wasn't just where I worked. It was my sanctuary. The place where I'd poured my grief and creativity. Knowing it had been infiltrated without my knowledge made me feel raw. Stripped bare.

The thought of someone spying on me was terrifying. The hairs on the back of my neck stood up just thinking about it. That was why I hadn't fought much when Callum demanded that I pack a bag and return to the Iron Rogues compound with him. I knew nobody could get to me there.

And I wanted to stick close to Callum. He was the only reason I wasn't spiraling right now. The calm in the storm I'd somehow found myself in.

It was a good thing he'd driven a truck instead of his motorcycle because I was too distracted to be a safe driver. My mind was still whirling when we reached the Iron Rogues compound.

He exchanged a look with the guy at the gate, who gave a quick nod before the heavy iron barrier rolled open.

When he pulled into the lot, I realized the place was bigger than I expected. The clubhouse had two stories, and there were other buildings, too. Not that I had a chance to look at them with how Callum rushed me into the clubhouse.

His fingers closed around mine as he helped me from the truck, and some of the tension in my spine unwound. More of my tension eased when he settled his hand against my lower back to guide me inside.

I kept my chin up as we walked through the door, ignoring the way a few men stopped what they were doing to glance our way. I reminded myself to breathe when Callum didn't slow down to answer any of the questions I could see in their eyes.

He practically dragged me through the large room, past leather couches and a long bar to head down a hallway and to a locked door. After unlocking and opening it, he stood aside so I could step in first.

I didn't know what I expected from his room, but it was tidy. Stark, even.

Dark gray sheets stretched taut across a king-sized bed, no wrinkles in sight. The walls were bare except for a single hook near the door. And a desk in the corner of the room.

A faint scent lingered in the air—leather, clean soap, and something spicy I couldn't name but immediately recognized as his.

When I stepped farther inside, I noticed a weathered paperback resting face down on the nightstand. The spine was cracked, and the cover was nearly worn off. I tilted my head to read the title. *The Old Man and the Sea.*

I hadn't read it, but the book seemed fitting for Callum.

I walked over to the bed and sat on the edge, my fingers curling around the end of the comforter. The mattress didn't give much beneath me.

Everything caught up to me at once. The hack. Ellen's disappearance. The bug. Yet I felt safe here. With Callum.

He crossed the room without saying anything, opened the closet, and set my suitcase inside. Then he carried my toiletries bag into the attached bathroom, disappearing for only a moment before returning.

"You can use anything in there." He gestured toward the door. "And there's space on the shelves for your stuff."

"Thanks." I looked up at him. "This is a lot."

His expression didn't shift, but something softened in his eyes. "You're handling it well, baby."

I'd never been close enough to a guy for him to give me a pet nickname, but I loved hearing Callum use one for me. It gave me the courage to admit, "Only because of you."

His hands fisted at his sides, his knuckles turning white and his nostrils flaring. "Fuck, baby. You can't say shit like that when we need to head down to Deviant's office."

My brows drew together as I asked, "We do?"

"He's digging into Ellen's disappearance and wants to see if she ever said anything to you that might send him in the right direction."

I stood, already moving. "Yeah. Of course. What-ever you need. I want to help."

His lips curved at the edges in a slight smile. "I had a feeling you'd say that."

Callum led me down another hallway, this one quieter and narrower than the one we'd used earlier to get to his room. Stopping at a closed door, he knocked once and opened it without waiting for a response. The guy at the desk looked up from his computer and gave me a quick once-over before shifting his gaze back to the man at my side. "I'm assuming you wanna stay for this."

Callum quirked a brow with a nod. "You'd be right."

"Mm-hmm." I didn't get the gleam of humor in Deviant's eyes, but it vanished quickly when he looked at me again. "Gemma, right? Come in and sit down. I'm Deviant."

"Nice to meet you," I murmured as Callum guided me over to one of the chairs in front of Deviant's desk. "I wish it was under better circum-stances."

"That's why I wanted to talk to you. So we can get to the bottom of Ellen's disappearance."

I glanced up at Callum, who stood behind me

like a wall of protection. "I'm willing to help however I can."

Deviant leaned forward slightly. "Not sure how much Hawk has told you, but your client Ellen hasn't just been reported missing. She's gone completely dark. Phone's off. Apartment's empty. No financial activity in the past forty-eight hours. Nothing."

My heart sank. "I hoped she was just...hiding or something."

"So did we." Deviant tapped a few keys. "That's why I need anything you can remember from your conversations with her. Even stuff that didn't seem important at the time. Something she said. The way she acted. Anything unusual."

"She mentioned going through a rough divorce not long ago."

"Yeah." Deviant nodded. "Already figured that out. I'm lookin' more for something that wouldn't be common knowledge."

I hesitated, sifting through my memory for anything that stood out to me. "She was nervous, but that's not unusual. A lot of women are at first. I do this whole routine to help break the ice—silly questions, stuff like 'are you the type who clears all your notifications, or do you have thousands of unread emails?'"

Deviant's fingers froze on the keyboard. "What did she say?"

"That she doesn't just clear them, she deletes messages constantly." I bit my bottom lip as I remembered exactly what she'd said. "And she also mumbled something about how that hadn't done much good in the past."

"Did you notice if her phone was rooted?" he asked.

I blinked. "I'm sorry—what?"

"Modified. Jailbroken. Anything off about it?"

"No idea," I admitted. "I barely saw it. She kept it in her bag for the whole shoot."

Deviant nodded and resumed typing at lightning speed. "Still helpful. Could mean she was paranoid about someone seeing something on her phone. Or that she was trying to hide her tracks."

I offered him a grateful smile. "I hope it helps."

"It does." Callum squeezed my shoulder before asking, "Need anything else?"

Deviant shook his head. "Not unless Gemma has more info for me."

"Nothing I can think of." I heaved a deep sigh.

"But I'll let Callum know if anything else comes to mind."

"That'd be good," Deviant murmured before his focus returned to his computer screen.

Callum tugged me gently to my feet, and I followed, the weight of Ellen's absence still pressing on my chest. The rest of the day passed in a blur. By the time we got back to his room, my head was heavy, and my nerves were frayed. But at least my belly was full of delicious food, and my heart was warmed by the welcome I'd received from everyone.

The door clicked softly behind us, and I kicked off my shoes before flopping onto the bed. I heard the low rumble of Callum locking the door, then his footsteps crossing the room. When I looked up, he was setting something down on the nightstand. My phone charger, which I hadn't even realized he'd grabbed from my bag.

"Thanks," I mumbled.

He let out a quiet grunt and sat on the edge of the bed beside me, his weight barely shifting the mattress.

The silence stretched, thick but not uncomfortable. It was strange how being near Callum eased something inside me. Like the frayed ends of my nerves were slowly stitching back together just because he was close.

"I've never stayed somewhere like this before," I said, my voice soft. "The clubhouse, I mean."

He shrugged. "Most people haven't."

"I thought it would feel...chaotic. Uncomfortable, even." I rolled onto my side so I could see his face better. "But it doesn't."

"No woman needs to worry when they're here." He stretched out next to me and interlaced our fingers. "Sure as fuck not you."

I rolled partway toward him. "Because of you?"

"Yeah, baby." He stroked his thumb against my palm. "It's safe to say that."

My breath caught, but before I could ask what that meant, he was moving. He turned toward me slowly, bracing one hand beside my hip and leaning in, giving me time to stop him if I wanted to. But I didn't. I wanted this.

"Say no if you're not ready after everything that happened today," he murmured, his words a hot puff of air against my lips.

I shook my head, barely whispering, "Please."

His mouth found mine in the next breath. He didn't rush the kiss. Instead, he devoured me with slow, unrelenting heat, like he had all the time in the world.

His lips moved with purpose, coaxing instead of taking, until I was clinging to his shirt. The room faded. The ache in my chest, the worry in my gut, the fear I'd carried for days—they all fell away. There was only Callum, and the way he kissed me like he'd been waiting for this moment for longer than he'd ever admit.

When we finally broke apart, both of us breathing harder than before, I couldn't stop myself from brushing my fingers over his scruffy jaw. His hand curled around the back of my neck, holding me in place.

We stayed like that for a long time, until he eventually broke the spell so we could get ready for bed. Where we just slept together...and nothing else happened. Unfortunately.

8

HAWK

Two nights. That's all it had been.

Two long, excruciating nights of holding Gemma in my arms. Of wrapping myself around her like a fucking shield and breathing her in while she slept.

Every time Gemma curled into me, her soft breath warming my throat, her thighs brushing mine under the covers, I came closer to snapping. I'd kiss her good night, low and deep, just enough to taste the sweetness of her lips. But then I'd pull back, bury my hunger, and clamp down on every possessive, mating-driven instinct in my body that told me to take what was mine.

Not yet.

She wasn't ready. And I wasn't going to ruin the safest place she'd ever felt by losing control.

Then I'd press my lips on her forehead or temple. Gentle and reverent. Sometimes it felt like that tiny touch was the only thing tethering me to sanity.

But it wasn't enough. It was never enough.

So instead, I worked.

Gemma was over at Blade and Elise's place, doing newborn pictures of their little girl, Emily. She said it would help her feel grounded, and I trusted Blade to watch her six while I handled the backend —sorting through Deviant's info dump, looking for anyone in Ellen's life who pinged the radar.

I was in my room at the clubhouse, my back against the worn leather of the desk chair and my laptop open in front of me. Multiple files from Deviant filled the screen. Each one was a carefully built profile of someone Ellen had regular contact with before she vanished.

Deviant was a genius with code and data trails, but he was a machine. Cold, technical, thorough. I was the one who read between the lines. Who knew how to strip someone bare from words unsaid and patterns that didn't make sense.

People were my specialty. I knew how to read

them. How to spot patterns, inconsistencies. And predators. So I was building a different kind of map. Psychological. Behavioral. Emotional.

I was mid-profile on one of Ellen's coworkers—a freelance designer who'd been a little too interested in her travel plans—when a knock on the door broke my focus.

I grunted a low, "Yeah."

Fox stepped in and tossed a package on the edge of my desk. I caught it before it slid off.

"Gift for your girl," he said as he dropped into the chair across from me and stretched out his long legs. "Don't say I never got you anything."

I peeled back the plain brown wrapping and leather met my fingers. Soft, deep black, unmistakably custom. I unfolded it and held up a vest in Gemma's size.

On the front, just above the left breast, it read Gemma. On the back was a patch with the club logo and Property of Hawk in bold block letters.

My gut twisted, and my heart thudded once —hard.

"Had Sheila start on it the day after we met her at the bar," Fox explained. "Figured you were already fucked, might as well make it official."

I looked up, one brow raised. "You always this optimistic?"

"No. But I know the look a man gets when his brain's stopped working and all that's firing is instinct." He crossed his arms. "You weren't thinking. You were reacting. You saw her, and that was it. Might as well save us all the wait."

I grunted. "You done waxing poetic about my woman?"

His grin was slow. "I'm just confirming what we all saw. You were hooked before she even said your name."

I didn't argue. Because it was true. And I didn't have the patience to pretend anymore. Instead, I traced the lettering on the vest, my thumb brushing over the word Gemma like it was holy. My jaw clenched.

"Thanks," I finally said.

"Just make sure she knows she's yours before someone else gets stupid." His gaze turned sharp. "That profile coming together?"

I turned the laptop, showing him the digital corkboard of notes, connections, and highlighted anomalies. "Almost. Got three possibilities I want to push harder on."

"Good." Fox nodded as he stood and headed for

the door.

He paused with his hand on the knob and looked back at me. "She's good for you. Makes you less of a cold bastard. Keep her safe."

"I will."

He nodded again and left, the door shutting with a solid click.

There was a reason I'd pledged my loyalty to him as president of the Iron Rogues. He was a fierce protector of those he considered family. He was always calm, always watching. A good man to follow and a lethal one to cross.

I stared at the vest for a long minute after the door shut.

It would look damn good on her. And I was determined to see her wearing it soon...with nothing underneath but my marks.

Before I got edgy and started pacing like a caged animal, I folded the vest and stowed it in the desk drawer.

Just in time because the door opened again. Tentatively, this time. And there she was.

My Gemma.

She stepped inside, cheeks flushed from the spring air. She wore a pale blue sundress that brushed her thighs and hugged her curves. A sweater was tied around her waist, her camera bag slung over one shoulder. Her hair was down, the soft waves brushing her chest, and my body heated with desire.

She looked like sin dressed in innocence.

I stood without thinking, my body moving toward her out of instinct.

"Hey," she said, her voice warm and sweet.

"Hey, baby." I reached out and took her hand, tugging her into the room. "Come here."

She melted into me instantly, arms wrapping around my neck as I walked her back to my chair and sat, pulling her down onto my lap. Her weight settled over my thighs, and I buried my face in her hair.

"You smell like sunshine."

She laughed softly. "That might just be baby powder. Elise had like ten different products in that diaper bag."

I chuckled against her neck, but the moment I heard her breath hitch, I pulled back. I saw it—the flicker of pain. The way her eyes snagged on my laptop screen.

The profile of Ellen was still open with a photo of her in the right corner. It was a cropped picture from the shoot, her smile bright and unaware.

Gemma went rigid.

Then a sob broke loose.

"I should've known or seen something. Maybe if I'd asked more questions or warned her to be careful or—" Her hands trembled as she pressed them to her face, her voice cracking. "She was sweet. I really liked her. Now she's just... gone. And I did nothing."

"Stop."

I wrapped my arms around her waist, pulling her close, burying her against my chest. Her fingers fisted in my shirt, and the raw grief shaking her made my heart ache in a way I hadn't felt in years.

"Don't do that, baby. This isn't on you," I murmured against her hair. "So don't you dare blame yourself. You didn't fail her. You were kind. You were good to her. That's more than most people ever give."

"But she trusted me."

"And you didn't betray that. The only person responsible is the sick fuck who took her. And they will fucking pay. I swear that on my life."

She trembled, another sob catching in her throat, and I held her tighter. Let her break. Let her feel everything she'd been trying to hold inside.

Tears soaked my shirt, and I held her until the shaking slowed. Until her breathing evened out.

But something had shifted between us. A crack

in the dam. A vulnerability so raw and open, it pulled my soul out through my chest.

When the crying slowed, I tipped her face up. Her eyes were red, lashes damp, mouth trembling. But she was still the most beautiful woman I'd ever seen.

When she leaned into me, I caught her lips with mine.

Not soft or tentative. This wasn't a kiss. It was a fucking firestorm.

She straddled my thighs, her hips rocking unconsciously, grinding that sweet pussy against the thick ridge of my cock. And I let her. Encouraged her, even. My hands slid down to her ass, kneading the firm curves and pulling her tighter, feeding the heat that was rising like a fucking inferno.

When I deepened the kiss, she gave a broken moan and melted into me.

And that was it.

9

HAWK

My control snapped.

"You feel that?" I growled against her lips, rutting my cock up between her thighs so she could feel the thick length of me through my jeans. "What you do to me?"

"Callum," she whispered, dazed and needy. "I can't—"

"You don't have to do anything but feel, baby."

My hands slid under her thighs, lifting her easily. I turned, carrying her to the bed in two long strides and dropping to my knees at the edge. I set her down gently, then I tugged the dress off, exposing her soft skin. Her bra followed, and my breath locked in my lungs.

She was fucking perfect. Full, heavy tits tipped

with dusky pink nipples already hardened from arousal. A soft belly that would soon be growing with our baby. And those sexy as fuck legs quivering as I stood over her, taking her in.

When I couldn't wait another second, I leaned down and kissed her throat, her collarbone, then trailed lower until I could wrap my lips around a flushed nipple and suck hard. Her back arched, her hands gripping my shoulders. I lashed the tight bud with my tongue while her fingers tightened, digging in. Then I switched to the other, and she cried out.

"That's it," I rasped. "Hold on, baby. I've got you."

"Callum..."

"Say it again," I growled, pulling back enough to watch her face.

Her lips parted. "Callum."

Hearing my name in her soft, breathy voice went straight to my balls.

I fisted the waistband of her panties and dragged them down her legs. Her scent hit me like a punch to the gut—sweet, earthy, and unmistakably aroused. And fuck, she was drenched.

"You're so wet already," I rasped, my voice rough with need. "That for me, baby?"

Cheeks flushed, she nodded and tentatively parted her legs a little farther.

My smile was wicked as I winked at her. "Good girl."

I made her come with my fingers first. One, then two, curling deep inside her while my mouth worked her tits again. She came with a gasp, trembling under me, her thighs clenching around my wrist as she fell apart.

Squeezing my eyes shut, I fought for control. When I opened them, Gemma was staring up at me in a daze, her chest rising and falling fast.

"You're untouched." It wasn't a question.

She swallowed hard, her voice barely a whisper. "Yes."

Pride and something primal surged in my chest. I braced my hands on either side of her hips. "Then listen close, Gemma. Because I'm only going to say this once."

She nodded, her eyes wide.

"This is mine. Your body. Your mouth. This sweet little pussy." I slid a finger between her folds and groaned when it came away dripping with her arousal. "It all belongs to me now."

Her lips parted, and her brown eyes darkened. A

breathless sound escaped her, a whimper and a plea rolled into one.

I lowered my face between her thighs and ran my tongue along her seam, groaning at the taste. "Fuck...knew you'd taste like heaven."

She cried out and fisted the sheets in her hands as her hips arched off the bed. I flattened my tongue and licked her again, then latched onto her clit and sucked hard. She screamed in ecstasy.

"That's it. Let go, baby. I want it on my tongue this time."

She trembled, thighs shaking, and then she shattered, moaning my name. I licked her through it and drank her down like a man starved.

Only then did I stand, unzip my jeans, and strip off my clothes. My shaft was thick, heavy, and leaking precome.

Gemma watched me, wide-eyed, her mouth forming a little O. When her gaze dropped to my cock, she gasped. "Oh..." She shook her head. "I can't —Callum, you're—"

"You can," I growled, crawling over her until she was pinned beneath me. "You were made for me, Gemma. This pussy? It's mine. Say it."

"I—it's yours," she whispered.

"Louder."

Her throat worked. "It's yours, Callum."

"Damn right, it is." Then I smirked. "Don't worry, baby. You were made to take me."

The head of my dick pressed against her slick entrance. I paused, closing my eyes for half a second, fighting for control.

My cock twitched, ready to plow into her untouched pussy, but I forced myself to breathe.

Then I pushed in. Slow. Steady. Watching every flash of emotion on Gemma's face. She bit her lip, eyes shining, but didn't look away. I groaned when her tight heat clenched around me like a vise. Inch by inch, I filled her until I hit that barrier that marked the end of her innocence. I leaned in and kissed her tenderly.

"This part's gonna sting," I murmured. "But I'll make it better real fast. Promise."

She nodded, barely breathing, pupils blown wide.

"I want you," she whispered.

"Fuck," I grunted. Then I thrust forward with one hard snap of my hips, burying myself to the hilt as her cry echoed off the walls.

Her nails bit into my back, and I stilled, staying deep while she adjusted. My breath was ragged against her neck. "You're mine now," I told her roughly. "And that means this is the only dick you'll ever have. I'm the first and the fucking last. You understand me?"

"Y-yes." The pain was finally clearing from her pretty brown eyes.

"No going back now," I growled. "You feel that? You're full of me, baby. Stuffed so tight you can't take another inch."

She relaxed slowly, hips tilting, legs wrapping around my waist. Then she whimpered, and her hips rolled slightly. "Please."

I fucking lost it.

I started to move, slow at first, dragging almost all the way out before slamming back in. The stretch, the heat, the feel of her clutching me like her body didn't want to let go. Fuck, it was better than anything I'd ever felt.

"Gonna ruin you for anyone else," I growled, driving in again.

My thrusts were deep and had her crying out with every stroke. I pinned her wrists above her head, grinding against her with every pump of my hips.

"Mine," I snarled against her mouth. "You're mine now. Say it."

"Yours," she choked out.

"That's right. My good girl. Gonna put a baby in you. Breed you. Fill that pretty belly with my kid."

Her breath hitched and her whole body arched under me, caught in some perfect storm of pleasure and surrender.

"You like that, don't you?" I rasped, gripping her thigh and hiking it higher. "Like knowing I'm gonna fill you up. That I want you knocked up with my kid. My baby in your belly so every motherfucker knows you belong to me."

Her inner muscles spasmed, and she moaned.

"You want it?" I demanded, my hips pounding into her faster now. "Want me to come inside you? Breed you?"

"Yes," she whimpered. "Callum, please."

I fucked her harder, my hips slamming against hers as I drove deep again and again, claiming her body in every way I knew how. Her nails dug into my back. Her moans turned desperate.

She screamed my name, and her eyes rolled back as her orgasm hit her hard. Her pussy clenched so tight I nearly saw stars.

The sounds of her pleasure sent me into a frenzy. My rhythm turned brutal, slamming into her again and again. Her moans blended with the slap of skin and the growl in my throat.

"One more," I demanded. "Want this pussy to take every last drop."

That was all it took to send her over the edge again, calling my name as she spasmed around me.

That was it. All I could take.

"Fuck, Gemma," I grunted. "I'm gonna come."

I grabbed her hips and pinned her down, before I drove into her one last time and exploded with a roar. I buried myself to the root as I spilled deep inside her, my entire body shuddering, my hips jerking as I emptied everything I had into her tight little pussy.

"Take it," I grunted. "Take every drop, Gemma. That's my seed in you now. My mark. You're mine. Stamped. Owned. Bred."

She whimpered, clinging to me, and I held her tight through every aftershock.

When it was over, I collapsed on top of her, caging her with my arms, careful not to crush her. She was panting, her body slick with sweat, and her eyes dazed.

I kissed her slowly, then brushed her damp hair back from her face and whispered things I never thought I'd say.

"Perfect. You're so perfect, baby. So good. So sweet. So mine."

She shuddered and held me tighter against her.

"You okay, baby?" I murmured, cupping her cheek with one hand.

She nodded weakly, a soft smile curving her lips. "That was...more than okay."

"Damn fucking right it was," I grunted, making her giggle, which made me smile.

I eased out of her slowly, then scooped her up and rolled us onto our sides, pulling the blanket up over us. She curled into me immediately, her head on my chest, hand over my heart as her breathing turned steady, and she drifted off.

I held her, one hand stroking her back, the other tangling in her hair. I lay there for a long time just staring at the woman who'd turned my world inside out. She was the future I'd never wanted. Until now.

She didn't know it yet, but I was already gone for her.

In too deep. Obsessed. In love.

And there was no line I wouldn't cross to keep her safe.

No sin I wouldn't commit.

No man I wouldn't bury.

Because she was mine.

And I never let go of what's mine.

I'd protect her with everything I had.

And destroy anything that dared come close.

10

GEMMA

Warmth anchored me before I even opened my eyes. A hard chest was pressed against my back, and a strong arm was slung around my waist. My neck was turned toward the heat, with my cheek resting against his ridiculously firm pec. The steady rhythm of a heartbeat thrummed beneath my ear.

It took a moment to remember where I was. And why I felt more at peace than I had in weeks.

Callum.

I didn't move, giving myself time to feel the soft sheets beneath me and the quiet hush of early morning. I dragged the clean scent of soap and leather that clung to his skin into my lungs.

For the first time in a long while, I wasn't afraid to fall apart. Wrapped in his arms, I knew I was safe.

My fingers moved without thinking, brushing lightly along the veins on the inside of his forearm where it rested against my ribs.

"I know you're awake." His voice was thick with sleep.

I smiled into his pec. "How?"

"Your breathing changed. And you've been tracing the same spot on my arm for the past five minutes."

"Maybe I'm just an active sleeper," I murmured.

"Not sure who's been lyin' to you, baby, but you sleep like a fucking log." His chest shook as he chuckled. "Except for the drool, you barely moved all night."

I twisted around to glare up at him. "I do not drool."

He swept his thumb gently across my bottom lip. "Guess you're right."

"There's no guessing about it," I grumbled. "And there hasn't been anyone to tell me how I sleep since I've never spent the night with a guy before, which you know after well..."

"You really gonna blush after I tasted almost

every inch of your body?" He dragged his palm down my back to cup my butt. "I only missed a few spots, but I'll make up for it later."

A shiver raced up my spine at his sensual promise. One that I sadly couldn't take advantage of now because we needed to stop by my studio to grab a few things before Callum got busy with work.

"I'm going to hold you to that."

"Good." He brushed his lips against mine. "We better get moving or I'll end up buried in you for the rest of the day. Your pussy needs a break after last night, and we have shit to do."

"Unfortunately," I grumbled as he rolled us out of bed.

We got ready to head out, with Callum ducking down to the kitchen to snag us some coffee. Mine was made exactly how I liked it, which I was still grinning over half an hour later when we climbed on his motorcycle to drive to my house.

I thoroughly enjoyed being wrapped around his muscular body. Wishing the ride was longer, I pouted as I tugged my helmet off.

Callum spotted my expression and shook his head with a deep chuckle. "Don't worry, baby. You'll be on the back of my bike as often as you want."

"Yay!" I did a dorky dance to celebrate.

"The only woman who's ever been there."

My heart swelled, but my good humor vanished when we turned the corner around the house, and I saw the entrance to my studio.

"Fuck," Hawk bit out, gripping my arm to pull me against his side. "Stick close, baby. I don't want you out here in the open while I get a closer look."

"Okay," I whispered, my stomach in knots as I took in the damage to my beloved space.

The outside of my studio looked like it had been through a war zone. Someone had smashed the exterior lights, and glass and plastic covered the ground. My flowerpots were shattered, and the soil was dumped everywhere. The bushes were hacked apart, branches splintered and strewn across the yard. Spray paint stretched across the pale blue siding in jagged, angry letters I couldn't even process yet.

But what stopped me cold were the scratches. Deep gouges were carved into the studio door. Unlike the paint, they couldn't be washed away.

I barely registered when Callum pulled me against his chest. My whole body had gone cold.

"I don't understand," I whispered against his shirt. "Why would someone do this?"

"I don't know, baby. But I'm gonna find out."

The conviction in his deep voice kept my tears at bay. At least for now. "Thank you."

"Stay behind me," he growled, releasing me only long enough to stride toward the door. His shoulders were tight, his spine was ramrod straight, and his steps were deadly quiet.

I wrapped my arms around my torso and followed, careful to stay close. The back of my throat burned as I spotted the broken pot that had once held a lavender plant from my mother's garden.

"They didn't go inside." Callum scanned the entrance with laser focus. "No damage to the lock. No breach through the windows."

I pressed my trembling fingers against my lips. "They came here to do all of this without even going inside?"

"They probably knew I upgraded the security," he explained. "Realized the bug was found and didn't want to risk getting caught."

"But they still did it. Because of me."

He turned so fast I flinched. "No, this is not on you."

"I should've—"

"Absolutely not," he cut in again, voice rising

with a fury I hadn't seen from him before. "You didn't do a damn thing wrong. They came after you, Gemma. And they're my fucking problem. Not yours."

Any trace of the calm, quiet man I'd woken up beside had been stripped away. Something lethal simmered just beneath the surface, and for the first time, I wondered what he'd do to the person trying to destroy my life. If he'd kill for me.

My breath stuttered.

His eyes locked on mine. "We'll burn this whole fucking town to the ground before we let anyone else be damaged because of this. You hear me?"

I nodded, unsure if I was more shaken by the damage or the intensity in his vow. A tiny flicker of fear curled in my belly, but it was quickly extinguished. Deep in my bones, I knew he would never hurt me or anyone who didn't deserve it. But there was no mistaking the edge in his voice. Or the way his eyes had gone cold and flat when he looked at the damage.

All that fury was for me, making me the safest person in Old Bridge because Callum wouldn't hesitate to destroy anyone who tried to harm me.

I was devastated, shaken, and exhausted, but I

took comfort in knowing that no matter what came next, I wouldn't be facing it alone.

The same couldn't be said for my clients, though. Until the guys figured out who was doing this, they could still be at risk. And they didn't even know it.

I turned slowly, taking in the wreckage one last time before whispering, "Should we call the police?"

His jaw tightened as he looked back at me. "No cops."

I wasn't surprised by his answer since he'd talked me into keeping them out of everything so far. But I still had to ask after what we'd found here today. And I wasn't as convinced now that they should still be kept out of it.

I heaved a deep sigh. "Okay."

"Stone will handle everything," he added, moving close again to wrap his arms around me.

"Stone?" I echoed. The name was familiar, but I'd met so many guys at the clubhouse that it was difficult to keep them all straight.

"He's the club lawyer, so he knows how to work the system better than any of us."

I felt a little better knowing Callum was getting their lawyer involved, just in case things somehow got even worse than they already were. Between Ellen being missing, the bug he found in my studio, and the destruction we were staring at, I didn't even want to consider what else could go wrong.

Almost as though he could sense the direction my thoughts had taken, Callum's arms tightened around me. "Stone is damn good at what he does. He's gotten some of my club brothers out of even more fucked-up situations than this before. And with Ellen missing, he'll be all in. We don't mess around when it comes to protecting people who need it. Club or not."

It finally clicked for me. The Iron Rogues wasn't just a motorcycle club. The guys didn't ask the cops for help because *they* were the help.

They handled things on their terms and in their own way. Fast and without all the red tape the police had to deal with.

I let out a shaky breath as the guilt I'd been carrying for dragging them into my mess began to loosen its hold. I hadn't asked for this level of protection, but they hadn't hesitated to offer it. Calling Lainie had been the best decision I could've made. I was lucky to have the Iron Rogues on my side.

And it had brought Callum into my life.

I leaned back to look up at him—this gorgeous but dangerous man who made me feel seen—and something inside me settled.

I wasn't alone. Maybe I never would be again.

Feeling a little lighter, I gestured toward the mess surrounding us and asked, "What about all this?"

He smirked. "One of the best parts of being an Iron Rogue...someone is always around to help clean up when shit goes down."

11

HAWK

The second I saw the state of Gemma's studio, I'd felt something split wide open inside me. The beast pacing just beneath the surface had surged forward.

My knuckles tightened around my phone as I stepped away from Gemma to call Maverick. She stood frozen beside me, her fingers trembling as she wrapped her arms around herself.

"You good?" Maverick asked when he picked up. He'd known where we were, so he probably assumed I wouldn't have a reason to call unless there was a problem.

"I need help with cleanup at Gemma's studio." My voice was low and even despite my pulse thundering in my veins. "Front's been tagged, lights smashed, and the yard is a fucking mess. They even gouged the door."

"You check the security footage?"

"No cameras caught it. Bastard knew we'd upgrade the system, avoided detection outside, and didn't step foot in the studio."

"Fucking hell. Okay, I'll get a few prospects out there and a couple of patches to supervise."

"Thanks. See if Stone is around. Going to need help keeping the police outta this shit."

"Done."

I hung up and stared at the vulgar streaks on the siding again, imagining how it would feel to slam the man responsible face-first into the concrete.

Gemma let out a shaky breath and stepped a little closer to me. I turned and pulled her back into my arms, inhaling deep to calm the heat boiling in my blood. Her eyes darted around, her mouth opening as if to say something, but nothing came out. She just buried her face in my shirt and took several deep breaths. But her attempts to calm herself didn't work, and when I heard her sniffle, I decided whoever had done this would suffer before he met his end.

Before we could say anything else, Stone pulled up on his hog. He dismounted slowly, like he had all the time in the world, but I knew better. Stone moved deliberately when he was sizing up a situation. Especially when he wanted the person responsible to sweat.

He took one look at the door, then glanced toward Gemma. "You call this in?"

"What do you think, asshole?" I snarked in a bone-dry voice.

Stone shrugged. "Just checking. Getting a feel for what I'm dealing with. I'll file a police report for the paper trail and insurance."

Gemma looked up at me. "I—should I have reported it?"

Before Stone could respond, I dropped my head so our faces were inches apart, forcing her to meet my eyes. "You don't call the cops, Gemma. You call me. And I was already here."

She blinked up at me, swallowing hard.

"I'll handle it. Always."

Stone made a sound like a dry chuckle. "You're his now, sweetheart. That makes you one of us."

Her breath hitched, her cheeks turning a soft rose. "I—I'm not—"

"Yes," I cut in, voice flat. Final. "You are."

She stared at me, lips parted, hope flickering in her eyes.

"You're mine, baby."

When I finally raised my head, Stone was smirking at me. "Better knock her up. Lock that shit down."

"Working on it."

Gemma flushed scarlet, the color flooding her from her ears down to her collarbone.

I grinned, but before I could say anything else, the rumble of bikes echoed off the buildings. Wrecker pulled up first, followed by Racer and a pair of fresh-faced prospects. They dismounted, eyes sharp as they took in the mess.

Gemma instinctively burrowed into my side, and I curled my arm tighter around her.

She knew they'd never hurt her, but they were still intimidating motherfuckers.

Wrecker sauntered over to us and caught her eye, giving her a rare smile. "Don't worry, darlin'. We've seen worse. This is nothing. Don't even have any blood to clean up."

Gemma stiffened, and I glared daggers at my brother.

"Appreciate you coming out," I said before he could say anything else stupid and force me to shut him up with my fist. Or my Glock. I was on the fence about that.

"No problem," he murmured, his humor dissi-
pating as his attention turned to the destruction.
"Told Mav we'd make it look like it never happened."

We got to work, and it helped keep me from
losing my shit, but the fire in my gut was growing by
the second.

I was dumping a load of trash into her bin when
my phone rang.

Not bothering to check who was calling, I
answered, "Yeah."

"I found it," Deviant announced.

"Found what?"

There was a short pause before he responded,
and I knew that meant it was bad.

"A hidden forum. Encrypted by invitation only.
Buried fucking deep on the dark web. There are
portfolios, private photo sets...all of them intimate
shots of men and women, or both. And a lot of them
are completely nude. Gemma's watermark is on at
least three of the boudoir samples."

"Portfolios? Samples?" My hand closed around
the edge of the trash can so tightly it cut into my
palm. "Why wou—" Then it hit me. "They're
fucking selling them?"

"It's a fucking black market. Voyeur shit. Pass-
word-protected trades, timed auto-deletes, rotating

proxies. Think dark web, but worse. Encrypted and buried behind dead-drop servers. Took me all night to crack. But I have a lead."

The world dimmed around me. All I could see was her face. That light in her eyes when she talked about helping women feel beautiful. About building something sacred.

And these fucking bastards had turned it into a market.

I didn't respond. I couldn't.

"I'll keep digging. I'll text when I have a trace on the account owner." He was silent for a moment before adding, "I should also warn you. I'm sure there are stolen photos from other photographers, but..."

My gut clenched at the anger vibrating in his voice.

"I don't think all of the photo shoots were consensual."

"What the fuck?" I breathed.

"I don't have proof with the professional pictures, but there is something about the expressions on some of these people. They can't completely hide the fear."

"You think they're being coerced? Blackmail?" I guessed.

Deviant sighed. "Or forced."

"Son of a bitch."

"Not all of the pictures are staged, though. It's obvious that some were taken when the subject had no idea they were being watched."

His words took a few seconds to sink in, then the fury I'd been stamping down broke through my carefully constructed barriers.

"What the fuck?" I roared.

"Keep it together, Hawk," Deviant snapped. "Gonna send your girl runnin' if you don't."

My teeth ground together until my jaw ached. Rage blistered inside me, stretching the edges of my control until it nearly ripped free. Deviant was right, but the beast inside me didn't give a shit. It wanted out. It wanted a fucking blood bath.

"Let you know when I have more, but you should get back here as soon as you can. Fox wants to strategize."

Then he hung up.

I stood there, breathing heavily and clenching my fists while I tried to find the strength to contain the monster once more. Gemma didn't need to see me like this. I didn't want her to.

Then behind me, Wrecker's voice cut through the haze. "You know why we call him Hawk, right?"

He had to be talking to Gemma.

Fuck!

"Because once he's locked onto a target, he doesn't blink. Never hesitates. Doesn't stop until the motherfucker is gone. Until the threat is eliminated."

There was a small gasp, and I froze. Afraid to turn around. To see her recoil. Worried I would see the trust in her eyes splinter.

But then I felt her steps behind me. Quiet. Steady. A second later, her hand curled gently around my arm. I turned, expecting distance, fear, or even disgust.

What I got was calm, reassuring brown eyes. Our gazes locked, and she searched mine for a second, then seemed to have a realization.

"I'm not scared of you, Callum," she said softly. "I could never be. I know you'll always keep me safe."

I didn't speak. I had no words to tell her what it meant to me to hear her say that. So I just pulled her into me and kissed her. One hand curled behind her neck, and the other gripped her waist. I didn't care who saw it. The whole damn street could stop to watch. I kissed her like I needed her breath to survive. Because I did.

And I needed her to feel it. Everything I couldn't say.

The claim. The promise. The fire.

We broke apart only when my phone buzzed with a text.

DEVIANT

> Get back to the compound now. I have what we need.

"We're leaving," I told her as I showed her the message. "The guys will finish the cleanup."

"But—"

"I need you with me, baby. Locked up tight behind steel and concrete. Otherwise, I won't be able to think straight."

She didn't argue. She never did when I put shit like that—knowing it wasn't up for debate when it came to her safety.

The moment we stepped into the lounge back at the clubhouse, chaos erupted.

Molly, Maverick's wife, burst out of the kitchen, baby on one hip, yelling over her shoulder. "Luna, if you eat that cookie, you're not getting another one!"

The three-year-old in question was already halfway behind the bar, crumbs trailing behind her like guilty glitter.

Molly groaned, catching her ten-month-old baby —Chase—just as he tried to wriggle free. She sighed when she saw us. "I swear, he skipped walking. Went straight to sprinting. I haven't sat down since."

Gemma laughed, and I felt some of the pressure inside me ease just a notch.

"I can help," she offered.

"You're an angel," Molly said, her face lighting up. "Seriously."

Before I stepped away, I leaned in and kissed Gemma's cheek. "This'll be good practice."

Molly burst out laughing. "Oh, he's definitely one of ours."

Gemma blushed hard but didn't have time to react further because Chase had wriggled free and took off like a rocket toward the hallway. Gemma darted after him, caught him mid-squeal, and the little punk smacked her cheeks with chubby hands and giggled hysterically.

"Up!" he shouted.

She laughed, heart-deep, as he wriggled and twisted, and I couldn't help the grin that tugged at my mouth. For one sliver of a second, I let myself imagine her like that—with our kid. Our chaos. Our joy.

I gave her a lopsided grin that made her eyes sparkle and kissed her once more. Then I turned and headed down the hall, where reality was waiting.

Fox's office was heavy with the kind of tension that soaked into the walls like smoke. The blinds were drawn against the afternoon glare, the only light coming from the overhead fixture above the round conference table and the glow of Deviant's laptop screen. The low hum of conversation cut off the second I stepped inside.

Fox stood near the table with his arms crossed, leaning against the edge like he'd been born there. Maverick sat across from him, one boot resting on the opposite chair, fingers steepled under his chin as he watched Deviant work. Midnight was off to the side near a small bar sipping coffee, his scarred knuckles drumming a rhythm against the counter.

Deviant didn't look up as I entered. He just kept typing, rapid-fire, muttering under his breath as code scrolled across his screen. I didn't speak until I crossed the room and stood beside the table, close enough to read the files flashing past his eyes.

"I want names. Now." My voice was low and even, but the tension in my spine didn't ease.

Fox nodded once. "You'll get them. Sit down."

I didn't. Couldn't.

Midnight raised a brow but didn't comment. Neither did Fox, though his eyes held a warning. They understood. Sometimes you needed to stay standing so the rage had somewhere to go.

Deviant finally stopped typing. He leaned back in his chair, stretching until his spine cracked. "Took some work, but I pulled the last-known backups off the cloud where the stolen photos were hosted. The metadata's scrambled to hell, but I recognized a few digital fingerprints from the hacker world."

My vision narrowed, a red haze crawling around the edges. "The ones helping him collect the photos?"

Deviant gave a slow nod. "Possibly. Or they work for the buyers. The black market collectors."

"What's the buyer list look like?" Maverick asked.

"Still tracing the backdoors. But the seller? That I got."

I crossed my arms and leaned forward, voice hard. "Who?"

Deviant spun the screen around. "Name's fake. But the IP that uploaded the files bounced through three VPNs and a Tor server before hitting a cloud storage address traced to a house outside Nashville. Belongs to a shell corporation, but guess whose name showed up on an internal transfer request last year?"

He clicked, and a face appeared.

My blood turned molten.

Darren Thomas.

Ellen's ex.

I gripped the back of the chair so hard I heard the wood creak. My molars ground together, rage clawing up my spine. It wasn't enough that he'd hurt

Ellen—he had to drag Gemma into it. Put her in his crosshairs like she was nothing but leverage.

"When I saw him, I went back to Ellen's phone and pulled more off her cloud backup. Stuff that hadn't synced to her visible folders. Like texts she'd deleted."

The words hit hard. I didn't move. Just stared at the lines of text now filling the laptop's display.

Deviant clicked to enlarge the file. "They're all from her ex."

I took a step forward. The room fell into a tense hush as the first message came into focus.

ASSHOLE EX

> You don't get to walk away. You think you can just erase me and start over? I was the only one who made you feel beautiful. You think someone else will lie to you like that?

Another pinged up as Deviant scrolled.

ASSHOLE EX

> You don't need other people telling you you're beautiful. That's just fishing for attention.

Then another.

ASSHOLE EX

You should be grateful I overlooked the things other guys would've walked away from. That's how much I love you.

You need me. Other men wouldn't have looked twice at you. I didn't care about all that. I chose you anyway.

You owe me, Ellen. I stuck around when no one else would have. Don't forget who made you feel wanted.

There's a difference between love and settling. You were lucky I never made you feel the difference.

I overlooked a lot because I loved you. That kind of patience doesn't come around twice.

You were never easy to love. I just never said it out loud.

The more I read, the harder my jaw locked, my pulse thudding behind my eyes.

The language was textbook control. Possessive. Threatening. The kind of psychological warfare that left invisible bruises.

But it wasn't just manipulation. It was a roadmap to violence.

"Here's the kicker," Deviant said as he brought up a screenshot of Ellen's phone calendar. "See this? After she added the appointment with Gemma to her calendar, she got one last text an hour later."

He clicked back to the messages.

> ASSHOLE EX
>
> Don't think I don't know where you are. I see you every time you step outside.

"Motherfucker's been watching her," I said, low and lethal. "Tracking her."

"Wasn't just watching," Fox said grimly. "He was targeting. This wasn't random. He thought this through. Wanted those photos. Wanted control of her."

My stomach dropped. "When he saw the appointment and decided to act."

Deviant nodded. "Day after the session, the texts started coming again."

> ASSHOLE EX
>
> You think you're some kind of model now? You're disgusting. Pathetic. No one's going to want you after they see what you really look like.

> You looked ridiculous posing like that. Like some girl playing pretend in a woman's body.

> You degraded yourself for a camera. Don't pretend it was for confidence or closure.

> You showed everyone what I had to put up with. All you did was prove me right—no one else would've wanted you if I hadn't made you feel like you were worth something.

> You should've been ashamed of that body, not showing it off like it's something special.

"Now he gets pissed," Deviant murmured as he kept scrolling.

"They always escalate," I said quietly, voice low and full of ice. "The moment she took control back, he had to remind her he still had power."

ASSHOLE EX

> You're not walking away from me. You're just dragging the leash until I yank it tight again.

> If you ever let another man touch you, I'll fucking kill him. You know I will.

Come back now, or I swear, I'll make sure no one else ever wants you.

Keep pretending you're free. I'll be the shadow you never see coming.

You're not brave. You're stupid. You'll get someone killed.

Smile for the camera all you want, bitch. I'll be the one waiting behind the flash with a bullet.

Midnight grunted in disgust. "I'd bet everything I have that he's the one who planted the bug. And vandalized the studio."

My rage wasn't fire. It was cold. Controlled. Deadly.

This wasn't just about Ellen anymore. This was about what *could've* happened to her. What might *still* happen to other women if we didn't end this. Because that was what men like him counted on— that no one would take these kinds of threats seriously until it was too late.

Maverick exhaled through his nose, sharp and measured. "This guy's got a god complex. He's been building this business for years—trading, threatening, maybe worse."

"He used Ellen's pain to justify his own sickness," I said. "Tried to twist it into something righteous."

Deviant nodded. "He didn't like that she posed for someone else. Even though he's been running this ring, he still couldn't handle her reclaiming herself."

"Fucking hypocrite," Midnight muttered.

Deviant's laptop pinged, and his fingers danced over the keyboard again. Then he leaned back, a slow grin curving his lips. "Got an alert for a recent log-on. Same alias. Same server. Different location."

"You get an address?" Midnight asked.

Deviant frowned at him. "Course I did, mother-fucker. I always come through."

Maverick rolled his eyes. "Just give us what we need."

"Southern edge of Nashville. Big place. Remote. Surveillance feeds off-grid, but I hacked a drone scan. Looks like a fortress, but not one we can't crack."

Midnight's voice was calm, but his eyes gleamed like frostbitten steel. "We hit it fast and hard."

Maverick shook his head. "We'll do recon first. Make sure the sick fuck is home and see if Ellen's there. If she is, we'll have to be more strategic than hitting it like a battering ram."

Fox pushed away from the table, walked around

his desk, and sat down. "Once you're in, take out the servers, rip up their network, do whatever it takes to wipe this shit out."

Deviant grinned. "I'll salt the digital earth."

"What about Darren Thomas?" Midnight wanted to know.

"He's mine," I snapped.

No one argued.

I nodded once, sharp and brutal. My fists itched for contact. "He's not walking away from this."

"Agreed," Fox murmured. "But he isn't the only one out there. He can point us to the other dealers and buyers. So he stays alive until we get answers."

As much as I wanted to put a bullet in the fucker the second I had him in my sights, I wasn't about to let any other depraved asshole get away with this shit if I could help it.

I nodded, then turned and headed for the hallway, not bothering to say goodbye. I didn't have it in me to waste words. Not when my girl's name had been dragged through a pit of filth and her work twisted into currency by a monster who should've rotted years ago.

When I found Gemma back in the lounge, she was crouched beside Luna, who was whispering secrets into her ear and giggling like they were plotting world domination. Chase had a cookie in one hand and was using the other to tug on Gemma's toffee-colored braid while babbling nonsense as she laughed. He made a move to take off, and she caught him before he could slip away again. "Oh no, you don't, little jackrabbit."

I watched her for a moment. The vision of her in the center of something bright, safe, and chaotic. A dream I'd never dared to want.

When I slowly crossed the room to her, my boots were heavy on the floor, and my chest was tight with something too big to name. Then I cupped her face in my hands. "Come with me."

Her smile faded at my tone. "What's wrong?"

"Nothing you need to worry about, baby. I just want you where I can see you."

I waited until she handed the little boy off to his mother, then I led her out, fast but not rushed, aware of every movement and every glance over her shoulder. When we reached my room, I scooped her into my arms before sitting in the desk chair and settling her on my lap.

"We've got a lead," I told her. "You don't need the details, but we're going after the people responsible. And I want you to stay here where you're protected."

Her brow furrowed. "Is it about Ellen?"

I hesitated. "Yes. That's why I need to go."

Her voice cracked. "Then let me come. If she's there—"

"No."

"Callum—"

"No." I grabbed her hips, eyes locked on hers. "This isn't up for debate. I need to know you're here where no one can get to you. I won't be able to breathe, much less focus if I'm worried about you."

Tears welled in her gorgeous brown orbs, but she nodded slowly.

"Thank you, baby," I murmured before I kissed her. It was dark and intense as I poured every violent promise and aching need into that one point of contact. When I finally pulled back, I wrapped my hand gently around the back of her neck and pressed my forehead to hers.

"He's not going to win."

Her throat bobbed. "But what if he already—"

"He won't, Gemma."

I kissed her forehead, then rested my lips on her temple.

"We'll end it. All of it."

Her lips trembled. "Come back to me."

"Always, baby."

13

GEMMA

"Staring at the door isn't going to make him get back any faster."

I swiveled my head to flash Molly a sheepish grin. "Is it that obvious?"

"Only because I've done this more times than I can count." Molly scooped Luna into her arms. "And I grew up in the life."

"Really?" I had gotten to know Maverick's wife during my time at the clubhouse, but I had no idea she and her sister, Dahlia—who was married to the Iron Rogue president—had been raised in an MC.

"Yeah, Dahlia and I are club princesses." She tickled Luna, her sweet giggles filling the empty space of the large lounge area. "Just like this little one, except our dad was the prez and hers is the VP."

"Which club?" I asked.

"The Silver Saints."

I nodded, as though the name meant something to me even though this was the first time I'd heard it. "Cool."

"So you can trust me when I tell you to find a good distraction because it's gonna be a long night," she recommended with a soft laugh as Luna's fingers wiggled under her chin.

Chase crawled across the black leather couch to get in on the tickling action, and inspiration struck. "Don't go anywhere. I'll be right back."

I raced up to Callum's room and stood in the doorway for a moment, taking in the space we'd shared the night before. It didn't make me miss him any less, but it helped me breathe a little easier.

I spotted my camera bag on the corner of his desk and crossed the room to grab it. The thought of pointing my lens at something innocent and full of life made me feel a little more like myself. I took one last glance around the space that had our things mixed. It wasn't nearly as tidy as it'd been the day Callum brought me here. And it definitely wasn't stark anymore. I liked that I'd brought some life into the room where he spent so much time.

With my camera secure in my hands and a quiet

determination building in my chest, I headed back downstairs. I couldn't be out there helping Callum and his club brothers, but I could capture the little moments worth protecting. Reminders of what they were fighting for while they were out saving Ellen.

By the time I made it back to the lounge, Molly was on the floor with Luna and Chase, their giggles echoing through the area like sunlight. Luna wore a sparkly tutu and mismatched socks, and Chase happily gnawed on the end of a spoon like it was the best teether in the world.

"Perfect," I whispered, slipping my camera out of the bag.

After removing the lens cap, I raised it to my eye and started snapping. Molly glanced up and beamed when she noticed me. Then she lifted Luna's chin with two fingers and whispered something that made the little girl tilt her head just so.

Her joy was effortless. And more beautiful than anything I had ever seen before.

Click.

Chase squealed and flopped forward onto his belly, kicking his legs like a swimmer while Luna jumped to her feet to twirl in a slow circle around him.

Click.

The tension in my shoulders began to uncoil. Capturing joy was something I could do. Documenting the pieces of life worth fighting for came naturally to me.

The sound of footsteps from the back of the clubhouse was followed by a familiar female voice. "Tell me I didn't miss photo time."

I turned to see Dahlia striding toward us like she owned the place. With good reason, considering who she was married to. Fox followed her, towering and tattooed, holding a squirming child in each arm. Their twins were the same age as Luna, and he made quite the picture carrying them, so I snapped a quick photo before they got too close.

"You're right on time," Molly called, grinning as Chase attempted to crawl into her lap while still clinging to his spoon.

"I told you she'd be shooting already," Dahlia said to Fox.

"How'd you even know?" I asked. "This was totally spur of the moment."

"That was me." Molly waved. "You're a photographer. It was easy to guess you went to grab your camera when you raced outta here like your feet were on fire but told me to stay put."

"Good point," I agreed with a soft laugh.

Dahlia grinned at me. "I hope you have a fast shutter. These two don't stop moving unless snacks are involved or they've passed out from sheer exhaustion. Which will hopefully happen in the next half hour, so they're not extra grouchy tomorrow morning."

"That ship has probably already sailed since it's already everyone's bedtime, but nobody is headed there anytime soon," Molly pointed out.

"Well, you're in luck," I replied, lifting the camera again. "I've trained on wilder creatures. Like bachelorette parties."

Fox chuckled before settling both kids on the rug. "They'll behave for a minute or two. Maybe."

"Two full minutes?" Molly teased. "Are you trying to spoil her?"

"I mean, she's family now," Dahlia quipped with a wink, then dropped onto the floor next to her sister.

Family.

It had been so long since anyone had considered me a part of theirs. I was honored that these amazing people thought of me that way, even if it was just because I was with Callum.

To stop myself from crying over how touched I was, I crouched again and framed the scene in my viewfinder. Fox's broad shoulders in the background,

Molly making Chase belly laugh, Dahlia brushing hair from Violet's forehead while Jett tackled a nearby pillow.

Click. Click. Click.

The sound of the shutter was steady and reassuring. An integral part of me.

Hope swelled inside me. I wasn't alone. Even with Callum gone, I had people around me who cared. Fierce, loyal people.

And no matter what came next, I'd have this moment captured forever. Proof that good things were still worth fighting for.

I snapped more than a hundred photos over the next twenty minutes, then Fox and Dahlia wrangled all four kids toward the kitchen for a bedtime snack.

Before the door swung closed behind them, Jett loudly declared his love for applesauce as Violet suggested they should hold out for cookies. Luna agreed with that plan.

Molly stayed behind. She didn't say anything at first, just sat down on the edge of the couch and tilted her head toward me with a knowing look. "You okay?"

I lowered the camera to my lap, brushing a lock of hair behind my ear. "Yeah. I'm just trying not to climb the walls while I wait. You were right about finding a good distraction. Maybe I'll go put on a movie when the kids are ready for bedtime."

"Running after Luna and Chase definitely makes the time fly by." She leaned back, arms stretched along the cushions. "But being with an Iron Rogue means you'll never face your fears alone. There are old ladies I can call who'd be happy to stay up with you for a movie marathon if you want."

My throat tightened. "That sounds really nice, but I'd hate to be a bother."

"None of them would think of it that way," she assured me.

"As an only child whose parents passed away a couple of years ago, it's hard to wrap my head around having a big family like this."

"As Hawk's woman, you're part of us now. But I get that it takes a minute to wrap your head around the way this life works." Her eyes sparkled with mischief. "Like the whole old lady thing. I know it might seem outdated or submissive, especially when we're dealing with other clubs who we aren't closely tied to."

"I'm not Hawk's old lady," I reminded her.

"It's only a matter of time, and not that much if I had to guess."

My cheeks heated, so I steered the conversation

back. "I've noticed the way you let the guys take the lead in public."

Molly didn't press when I dodged talking about my relationship with Hawk. "That's by design. When you're out there with your man's property patch on your back, you let him run the show. It keeps things smooth with other clubs and maintains the image. But behind closed doors, us women run our damn kingdoms. Don't let the leather, hogs, and tattoos fool you. These men worship their women. They just don't want anyone else thinking they're easy to mess with. Their badass reputation keeps us all safe."

That earned a small laugh from me. "So you're saying I don't have to stay quiet and sweet all the time?"

"Hell no," she replied with a snort. "Just be smart about when and where. You've already got Hawk wrapped around your finger anyway."

Heat rushed to my cheeks again. "I don't know about that."

"Oh, trust me." Molly sat forward to tap my knee. "That man would light this whole town on fire for you."

I looked down, twisting my fingers in my lap. "That's kind of what I'm scared of."

Her expression softened instantly. "Not because you think he'd hurt you, though."

"No," I quickly confirmed. "Never. It's just that I've never had someone care that much before."

She flashed me an understanding smile. "You're not weak for leaning on him. None of us are. These men don't want fragile. They want fierce. But they also want to be your safe place."

I swallowed hard. "I want to be that for him, too."

"Then you will be." Molly smiled, eyes crinkling. "Just by loving him the way only you can."

Her advice stayed with me all night long while I waited for Callum's return.

14

HAWK

The roar of six Harleys split the night as we tore down the highway just south of Nashville. The wind ripped at my cut, flapping the leather against my back as the city lights disappeared behind us. Every breath I took was thick with the scent of damp asphalt, pine sap, and gasoline. But none of it cut through the rage burning in my chest.

We rode in tight formation. Storm, as our Road Captain, was at the front. Maverick and I were at his flank, with Blade, Racer, and Wrecker just behind us.

Storm's silhouette blurred in the dark, and Maverick rode like the road bowed beneath his wheels. These weren't just my brothers. They were predators. And tonight, we were hunting.

At the edge of the city, we veered off the highway and rolled down a quiet residential street, then rumbled to a stop in the gravel drive of a small craftsman-style home. It belonged to one of Deviant's contacts—a quiet tech guy who owed us more favors than he could count. We parked the bikes out of sight, ditched the open gear, and loaded into two matte-black surveillance vans. I climbed in with Storm and Maverick, and the doors shut behind us with a dull thunk.

The smell of oil, leather, and gunpowder filled the cramped van. The air inside was thick with tension, and Maverick was the first to break the silence. "You look like you're ready to snap someone's spine with your bare hands."

I didn't glance up from the fresh magazine I was sliding into my Glock. "That's the fucking plan."

Storm snorted from the driver's seat, hands light on the wheel like he was back in the desert. "Try not to shoot Darren until we find the servers."

"Or Ellen," Maverick added, fitting his comm into place. "Let's not forget the point of this."

"She's first priority," I growled.

The comm cracked to life. "Boys," Deviant said, smooth and dry, "you're on camera. Mansion's lit like a Vegas high-roller party. I count three dozen guests already. More arriving."

"Status inside?" Storm asked.

"Security's thick but sloppy. Standard body-guard rotation. No sight of Ellen yet, but I've been watching that kitchen elevator. It goes somewhere I can't follow on the security cameras. Has to be underground. That's where the rot is."

"Time to play nice," Wrecker said from the second van. "Been too long since I busted down a rich prick's door."

"Or blew one off the hinges," Racer added dryly, making Wrecker chuckle.

"Definitely in the mood to drop an entitled bastard on his ass," Storm drawled.

Maverick snorted. "I'd throw him through a wall."

"Save the party tricks, boys," Blade chimed in calmly. "Make sure Ellen walks out first."

We parked two blocks from the mansion. Far enough to keep off the radar but close enough to move fast. The vans sat in the shadow of a hedge-lined property, engines ticking as they cooled.

My fists clenched as one car after another glided around the circular drive. Sleek limos and polished Town Cars. Men in designer suits stepped out, escorted by muscled bodyguards. Some had women on their arms—gorgeous and glittering as their diamonds caught the porch lights. They were more jewelry than clothing. None of them looked down. None of them knew or cared what they were walking into.

The time passed slowly while tension coiled around my shoulders. Every car that arrived ratcheted the pressure tighter, making my jaw tighten.

When Darren finally stepped out of his black Town Car at eleven sharp, surrounded by other smug bastards with snakeskin shoes and crooked smiles, I stilled. My blood went cold.

"That's him," I said flatly. "That's the sick fuck."

"Confirmed," Deviant said in my ear. "Still no sign of Ellen. But the elevator? Guests go down. Most don't come back up."

Silence stretched for a beat, then Maverick said, "Send in Storm."

I jerked my head toward him. "No. I go."

Maverick didn't look away from the monitors. "Not a chance. You'll rip him apart before we know where Ellen is. You want it done clean? Let him ghost it."

Storm clapped a hand to my shoulder. "You're better on breach anyway."

I didn't like it. But they were right.

Ghost it—yeah. That was what Storm did. He melted into the shadows, silent as sin. And as much as I hated not being the first one through the door, I knew Maverick and Storm were right.

Fifteen minutes later, he came through the comms. "Got her. Second-floor bedroom. Out cold. Lingerie. Lights and a camera. That son of a bitch was photographing her."

"Get her out," I growled. "Now."

Ten minutes later, Storm reappeared from the far side of the house, cutting through shadows while cradling a limp, unconscious Ellen in his arms. She looked fragile and pale, her limbs slack and her breath shallow. Blade opened the van doors and took her gently, checking vitals.

"She's sedated but stable," he confirmed. "We should get her to the hospital as soon as we're home, but she's not in immediate danger."

Storm's face was carved from stone. "This isn't just a voyeur ring. I heard one guy talking. Darren gave him a pickup receipt. Said his purchase would be ready tomorrow."

"Photos don't need pickup dates," Maverick muttered.

"No, they don't," I growled.

"Whatever's in the basement," Racer added. "It's got to be there. And it's something much damn worse."

No one disagreed.

Maverick's jaw clenched. "Let's get this shit show on the road."

"Time to go loud?" Wrecker asked.

"No," I disagreed. "Time to go fucking deadly."

We breached the mansion through the front, and I was first through the door—silent, lethal, purposeful. The scent of old money hit me the second I crossed the threshold.

The entryway glittered with opulence—crystal chandeliers and marble floors. A grand staircase rose through the center. Music played somewhere—jazzy and hollow, trying too hard to feel expensive. It was paired with the low murmur of conversation and clinking glasses. A party, but not the kind that deserved to end with dessert.

"Can't see him on camera this second," Deviant said over the comms. "But he was in the kitchen five minutes ago and hasn't popped up on any other camera since."

We moved like a unit. Maverick swept left. Wrecker peeled right. Storm and I made a beeline for the kitchen.

I stalked down the hall with a predator's calm, the weight of my knife and Glock as natural as the leather cut on my back. Suddenly, a man stepped out of a room and turned our way.

There he was. Darren. The vile excuse for a human.

Before he realized what was happening, Storm quickly stalked over and pressed his gun firmly to the bastard's temple. I followed more slowly, my boots silent on the tile, and my rage coiled tight.

"Move," I snarled at the little shit.

Storm shoved his gun harder into Darren's head and herded him toward the kitchen.

Darren's eyes were wide, and my nostrils flared at the smell of the anxiety bleeding off him.

The kitchen was all sleek steel and gleaming granite. Cold. Sterile.

Thanks to the blueprints of the mansion Deviant had acquired, we went straight to a hidden set of doors behind a stainless steel cabinet. They led to a small corridor, and the elevator was recessed in marble at the end of it.

A sleek keypad blinked beside it, next to a biotech scanner.

"Retinal scanner," I told Storm as I examined the device.

Darren froze and stammered, "You don't know what you're doing."

Storm leaned in, breath hot on the back of his neck. "Scan your damn eye. Or I'll take it out of your skull."

Darren whimpered and pressed his face to the scanner. The panel beeped, turning green. Then he just stood there as if he was waiting for instruction.

"Now the code," I said, low and deadly.

"No," Darren spat. "I'm not—"

"Eight. Three. Seven. Four. Two," a calm female voice interrupted.

All heads snapped toward the entrance to the hall.

A woman stood in the archway in a red dress cut down to her navel. Flawless makeup. Glittering jewels. Stilettos. But her face was like marble. Her eyes...they were dead. Except when she looked at Darren. Then loathing practically lit her up from the inside.

"He gave it to me once. Thought it made him important," she said coolly. Then she looked at Storm. "Don't let him die quickly and make it damn painful."

Before anyone could respond, she vanished.

Storm shoved Darren against the wall. "You heard the lady."

His face twisted with anger, Darren punched in the code and the elevator doors opened.

Maverick and Wrecker appeared then, both wearing furious expressions, their hands gripped tightly around their Glocks.

Maverick motioned to Storm. "You stay up here. We'll see what's on the other side."

Wrecker cracked his knuckles. "About time."

I stepped in last, and the door closed as a soft mechanical hum began. As we descended, the air turned colder. When the doors opened, a hallway unfurled in front of us. Pale concrete under harsh fluorescents. Long, curved, and lined with identical black, narrow doors. A chill crawled down my spine.

"What the hell is this," Maverick muttered, jaw tight.

"Deviant," I said into my comm. "You seeing this?"

Nothing. Just static.

"We're on our own," Maverick said grimly, tapping his earpiece. "Comms are jammed."

Taking a step closer to the nearest door, I tried the handle, but it was locked. They all were.

Wrecker swore under his breath as we followed the curve. "There's something in the middle that these all open up to. Has to be."

I didn't say anything. I just kept moving, tugging every handle until one of them finally gave way.

Glancing over at Wrecker, I jerked my head toward the door, and he nodded.

Maverick and I stepped back and waited, guns at the ready. Wrecker yanked the door open, and I went in first, silent and alert.

The room was dark, with walls lined with leather panels. In the center was a man in a navy suit, lounging in a plush leather recliner like he owned the world. A low table beside him held a crystal glass, half full. A remote rested in his hand.

On the far wall, I saw what looked like a viewing window, but it was opaque and flickered to life as the man pressed the button on the remote. It lit up with images—bodies. Screen after screen of nude or barely covered females. All with blurred faces and watermarked with serial codes and timestamps.

Son of a bitch.

It was a fucking catalog. Women indexed like objects.

I cursed, and the man turned, startled, as if annoyed by the intrusion. When he saw us, his eyes flickered to the far corner, and a shadow peeled out of it. A bodyguard in black, big and fast.

But I moved faster.

Two steps forward, pivot, elbow to the throat, twist the wrist, disarm. I caught the knife midair, reversed it, and buried the blade in the guy's shoulder. A twist, a grunt, and the guard dropped.

The man in the suit scrambled to his feet, hands shaking, and backed against the wall.

"Please," he gasped. "I didn't—"

He lunged for a switch. A panic button.

I didn't hesitate. One bullet. Clean. Right between the eyes.

The screen flickered, then went dark.

Something icy spread through my veins. A sense of foreboding.

Then a speaker crackled above our heads. "Tonight's auction will begin in sixty seconds. Digital transactions will resume after the live segment concludes. Please place your bids promptly. Our merchandise moves fast."

My stomach clenched.

A room lit up on the other side of the window. A quick glance around showed that the walls were all lined with one-way glass.

The room went dark again for half a minute,

then a spotlight shined down in the very center of the room. A woman stood under it, naked but for a G-string and a lace bra. She slumped on trembling legs in five-inch heels. Her eyes were wide with fear but unfocused. Sedated.

"What the fuck," Wrecker breathed.

A disembodied voice began to chant numbers. "Ten thousand." A bell chimed. "Twelve." Another ring. "Fourteen. Do I hear sixteen?"

With each ding of the bell, the number rose. A new bid.

I couldn't breathe.

It was a fucking auction.

My fists clenched so tight my bones ached. Rage coiled in my chest like a blade waiting to be unsheathed.

The lights dimmed. A final bell. "Sold."

Darkness descended briefly, then the room lit up once more.

This time, it was a man. Young. Barely fucking legal. Wearing only a Speedo. Arms limp and mouth parted like he couldn't quite understand what was happening. Just as drugged. Just as humiliated.

"They're not only taking pictures of them," Maverick said, his voice a growl. "They're selling them."

"They're selling people?" Wrecker hissed.

"They're trafficking," I corrected. "Fucking monsters."

I was stunned by this revelation. A fucking human trafficking ring, disguised under pixelated filth and dark web encryption.

Wrecker was already gone, pounding back into the hallway. "Gonna find the holding room."

Maverick made for the landline in the corner. Old-fashioned rotary, red. The kind used for panic calls or locked systems.

He picked it up, dialed a number, and waited.

"Who're you calling?" I asked, still staring at the screen.

"Backup," Maverick answered. "Local associates. Be here in ten. Not gonna handle this one alone."

I nodded slowly, a brutal smile tugging at the corner of my mouth. "I'm going to see what's left of Darren."

The moment I reemerged from the elevator, the fury came with me. The air upstairs felt thicker than before, as if the whole mansion had absorbed the stench of what we'd uncovered below. Behind me, the walls were still echoing with the ghosts of the auction. Glass rooms. Drugged bodies. People being bid on by monsters in designer suits.

I thought about Gemma. Wondered if this was where she would have ended up if she'd never called Lainie. Immediately, I shook the thought away. It would only lead to death and destruction. If the beast was released, no one would get out alive.

I focused on an image of her seared into my memory—safe in my bed, sleepy and satisfied. Staring up at me with those soft brown eyes, her tempting lips curled in a sweet smile.

I stalked through the corridor, boots heavy on polished hardwood, my fists clenching with every step. The walls vibrated faintly, with music still playing somewhere in the house. It grated on my already frayed edges.

Racer waited in the hall, his expression as hard as granite. "Storm's got him in the guest suite, end of the hall," he muttered, motioning with his chin. "Didn't want him near the kitchen. Too many knives."

Good. I wanted to bleed Darren somewhere quiet.

I didn't knock. Just shoved the door open with the heel of my hand and stepped into the room like the devil had come to claim Darren's soul.

The bedroom was plush. Gold accents, silk curtains. Velvet chairs arranged near a crackling gas

fireplace that tried to pass as elegant but felt staged—
like everything else in the house.

Storm stood calmly to the side, one hand
wrapped around his gun, the other resting casually
on the back of a high-backed chair. Darren Thomas
sat trembling on the cushion. He was bound, bruised,
and already bleeding from a split lip and swollen eye.
His tailored suit was wrinkled, the collar torn, and
sweat plastered his thinning hair to his forehead.

The moment I walked in, Darren tensed.
Coward.

But it wasn't him that stopped me in my tracks.

It was the wall.

Six framed photographs lined it in staggered
columns. Boudoir portraits, blown up and printed in
high gloss. Women in lace and satin posed artfully,
unaware their beauty had become part of a predator's trophy room.

And there—centered, larger than the rest—was
Gemma.

My Gemma.

She stood barefoot, back arched slightly, hair
tumbling down over one bare shoulder, the lighting
caressing her skin. So beautiful. Confident. But still
vulnerable.

And framed like a fucking trophy.

Something inside me shattered.

I didn't even register crossing the room. One second, I was frozen—shocked and hollowed out by the image of her. The next, I was across the floor, fists buried in Darren's face, blood flying like flecks of rust across white walls.

Storm didn't interfere. Not at first.

I wasn't gentle. I wasn't quiet. Snarling sounds tore from my chest, and I felt the pressure leave me every time my knuckles cracked bone. Darren's head whipped back and forth under the barrage, blood splattering onto the armrest, the floor, and the sleeves of my shirt. He wasn't fighting back. Couldn't.

I kept going, and the beast was finally free to rain down hell. A bone snapped, and Darren screamed through broken teeth.

Storm finally stepped forward, voice calm but edged with warning. "Brother."

I kept going, kneeing the chair, rocking it back so Darren flailed, wheezing through a broken nose and split, swollen lips.

Storm let me continue until Darren barely breathed.

Then he caught my wrist. "Enough."

It wasn't a request.

"Not yet," I growled.

Storm didn't blink. "Need his face at least partially intact. For now."

Slowly, deliberately, I lowered my hand.

Darren was barely conscious as he slumped to the floor. His face looked like raw meat—eyes swollen shut, lip shredded open, blood soaking the front of his shirt. He moaned in short, shallow bursts. Pitiful and weak.

Storm pulled him upright with one hand and shoved him back in the chair.

At that moment, the door creaked open again.

Maverick walked in, took one look at the scene, and exhaled a slow sigh. "Couldn't have left *one* cheek untouched," he muttered, glancing at Darren's obliterated face. "Gonna take a day or two before he can form words again."

I shrugged, flexing my blood-slick fingers. "Doesn't need words. Needs to remember pain."

Maverick met my eyes across the room, but there was no judgment. Only approval.

"We'll get what we need out of him once Blade takes care of the swelling. He'll talk. Eventually."

"Gonna make fucking sure of it," I said, low and brutal.

Maverick nodded. "Backup is arriving now. Storm, you and Racer move the victims to a bedroom upstairs. Find them some clothes. Wrecker and I locked the customers in the viewing area." One corner of his mouth lifted. "Told 'em we were putting them up for auction as bitches to the nearest prison."

Storm snorted, and Racer coughed a laugh. Any other time, I'd have appreciated the levity in a destructive situation like this. But the only thing on my mind was Gemma. I needed her in my arms. Needed to be inside her. To remind myself that she was real. Safe. *Mine.*

"Hawk," Maverick said, his voice dipping. "You good?"

"No," I replied honestly. "But I will be. I'm going home."

Mav's eyes narrowed slightly, studying me. "To Gemma?"

"Where the fuck else?" I snapped.

"Just makin' sure you weren't planning to camp out in The Room until your punching bag arrives."

I grunted. "Not worth being away from my woman."

"I hear that," Storm muttered.

Crossing the room, I paused to look once more at

Gemma's framed photo. She didn't belong on this wall. Not in this nightmare.

I took it, removing the frame so I could keep her close to my heart.

And left Darren in the wreckage of his sins.

15

GEMMA

The scent of cinnamon and brown sugar clung to the air, warm and comforting, even though my nerves were anything but. I hadn't slept more than a couple of hours, too keyed up to rest while Hawk was out doing whatever it took to bring Ellen home and take down the man behind it all.

I finally gave up and crept into the clubhouse kitchen just after four, preheated the ovens, and started working. The coffee was already brewed, and three French toast casseroles bubbled inside the oven.

Callum had texted about an hour ago to let me know they were headed back. A hot breakfast was the least I could do for the guys after they'd been out all night to help me.

I sat at one of the long tables, stirring creamer into my coffee. Keeping my hands busy helped, but the waiting was finally over.

The kitchen door creaked open behind me. I turned and got the best surprise.

Callum.

The second I saw him, I forgot all about French toast and coffee.

He looked freshly showered, dressed in a clean black tee and worn jeans. His hair was slightly damp, flattened at the top and curling slightly at the ends, like he'd shoved his helmet on while it was wet. His dark eyes were steady as he crossed the room.

I slammed my mug onto the table, jumped to my feet, and met him halfway. "You're back!"

His arms wrapped around my waist, and he lifted me off my feet. When he set me back down, he reached for my hand, curling his fingers around mine with a quiet intensity that made my heart skip.

Without a word, he turned and guided me out of the kitchen. "Where's everyone else? I hope nobody got hurt."

Callum shook his head. "All of our guys are fine."

Fox walked toward us, shaking his head. "Except Wrecker." At my look of concern, he added, "Not

'cause he got hurt. Just pulled away to handle something that I have a hunch is gonna rock his world."

"French toast casseroles are in the oven and only
need a few more minutes," I called, wondering what
he meant by that as Callum tugged me away.

Fox nodded. "I'll make sure they get pulled out
before they burn."

Callum led me toward his room. The door shut
behind us with a soft click, and it was finally just the
two of us. Callum turned toward me and pulled
something from the inside pocket of his leather cut.

A framed photo. Mine. Another one from my
archive. Soft lighting, lace-trimmed lingerie, and that
vulnerable strength I tried so hard to capture in
others—reflected in me. The kind of photo I never
would've shared publicly even though it was
beautiful.

My breath caught. "You found him. Is Ellen
okay?"

"Yeah, she's good now." He pressed the photo
into my hand. "This was the only copy he printed.
Deviant scrubbed everything digital. There are no
backups. Nothing on the cloud. No drive that
someone is gonna find. Just this, and now you
have it."

"Thank you." I was touched by the fact that he

knew me well enough to understand that I needed to have this copy. Just like I knew he would've wanted to destroy it in a rage. But he held back to give me what I needed. "I love you."

His expression sharpened, his eyes turning fierce. Then he stepped in close, cupping my face in his big palms. "You're mine, Gemma. Forever."

I blinked up at him, even as butterflies took flight in my belly. "That's it? I was kind of expecting to hear those three little words back from you."

His lips twitched. "I can do better than that."

He strode over to the desk, yanked open a drawer, and pulled something out. My breath caught in my chest when I realized what it was. A black leather vest in my size, with a property patch on the back announcing to the world that I belonged to Callum.

"Be mine, officially. Be my old lady."

He held it out with both hands, and my throat closed up. My fingers curled into the leather as I clutched it against my chest.

"I love you, Gemma," he said quietly but without hesitation. "You're it for me."

Emotion swelled in my chest. "Yes. So much yes."

"Gonna slide a ring on your finger soon, too," he promised before hauling me against his chest.

His mouth crashed into mine, and everything else faded. There was only us.

The warmth of his body. The leather of the vest pressed between us. The way his fingers curled around the back of my neck as though he couldn't bear to let me go.

I dropped the vest onto the edge of the bed without breaking the kiss. My hands gripped the front of his tee, twisting in the soft fabric as he angled his head and deepened the kiss, stealing the air from my lungs.

His fingers slipped beneath the hem of my shirt and dragged it over my head in one fluid motion, eyes darkening as he looked at me.

"Lie back, baby."

I obeyed, heart thudding against my ribs as I scooted onto the mattress. He followed me down, bracing his weight above me with one arm while his other hand skated over my side and down to my thigh.

"I need you," I whispered.

"You've got me." He dipped his head and brushed a kiss over my collarbone. "Always."

He quickly finished undressing me, then his

boots and jeans hit the floor. I stared as he stripped out of his cut and shirt, exposing his muscular chest to my hungry gaze. I licked my lips when he shoved his boxer briefs down his thick thighs, and his big dick sprung free, a drop of precome already beaded at the top.

Callum fisted the shaft, stroking up and down. "Is my baby hungry for me?"

"Always."

His dark eyes heated even more. "Not sure I have it in me to feel your sweet lips wrapped around my cock without blowing tonight."

"The blow job can wait." I trailed my fingers down the valley between my breasts. "We have all the time in the world for everything we want to do to each other, right?"

"Damn fucking straight we do," he growled.

Then he was on top of me, skin to skin, all heat and muscle. His hands skimmed up my sides, his mouth moving across my chest in a worshipful path that quickly had me writhing beneath him.

"Gotta get you ready to take my cock, baby."

He wedged his broad shoulders between my thighs so he had better access to my pussy. After lowering his head, he ate at me like a starving man. Licking between my pussy lips and circling my clit with his tongue. His touch was warm and wet, hitting the perfect spots over and over again.

Arching my hips off the mattress, I rode his face until he pinched my clit and waves of pleasure crashed over me. "Yes, oh yes! Callum!"

When I finally stilled beneath him, he lifted his head. "Fucking love to hear you cry my name like that. Best damn sound in the world."

He notched the tip of his dick at my core, but I gripped his veiny forearms to stop him before he sank inside me. His gaze swept over my expression before he asked, "What's wrong, baby?"

"Absolutely nothing," I assured him with a hazy grin as I wrapped my legs around his waist. "It's just that I want to be on top."

"Hurry, baby. I need you," he rasped, rolling us over so I was straddling him.

The need in his deep voice spurred me on. I lifted and positioned his dick at my entrance, and he wrapped his hands around my waist to steady me. I glided my pussy down his hard length, getting it wet.

"Take what you need, baby," he urged as I slowly lowered myself until he was deep inside.

I swiveled my hips. "Wanna drive you wild."

Callum stroked one of his palms up my spine to tangle it in my hair. Tugging my head back, he punched his hips up, going even deeper. "You always do. Never gonna get enough of this sweet pussy that's mine. Only ever mine."

The possessive thread in his tone ratcheted my desire even higher. Then his other hand slid between us, and he circled my clit with his thumb. "Ride me, baby."

I might've been on top, but he was still in control. Which somehow made me feel even more free as I let go, gliding up and down his hard shaft until my body was strung taut above him. "So close."

"Fly apart for me," he grunted, yanking me down against him so his dick was anchored deep.

I ground up and down as much as I could with how he was holding me, my breasts bouncing while I flew apart. He followed with a groan that sounded like my name and a vow all in one. "Gemma, fuck yeah. That's it, milk the come from my cock."

My orgasm went on and on until I finally collapsed against his chest, fully spent.

Sprawled against him with his arms wrapped around me, I knew exactly where I belonged.

Forever.

EPILOGUE

HAWK

I waited just outside the door of Gemma's studio until the light I'd installed beside it turned from red to green. Then I knocked. Gemma's sweet voice floated to my ears, telling me to come in.

We'd set up this system so I would know when she was in session and couldn't be disturbed. When the light was green, it meant I could knock, but she only called for me to enter if the client gave her permission.

The bell above the studio door chimed just as I stepped inside. The low, delicate jingle barely cut through the quiet hum of soft instrumental music drifting through the space. A warm, clean scent mixed with hints of floral curled in the air—Gemma's signature. Familiar and comforting, it wrapped around me like her touch.

Sunlight slanted through the front windows, filtering through gauzy curtains and glinting off the framed prints lining the wall. Soft, tasteful boudoir shots in black and white, angled just enough that nothing was exposed, but everything was suggested. Confidence, power, and vulnerability created into art.

At the far end of the space, Gemma was whispering with a client as she slipped into a jacket. The woman was glowing from the shoot, her eyes lit with a new kind of confidence. Her smile was wide, grateful, and real. She touched Gemma's forearm gently—almost reverently—before murmuring her thanks and heading for the door.

I stepped aside to let her pass, holding the door as I dipped my head in greeting. The woman flushed but didn't look embarrassed—just empowered. Gemma had that effect on people. On the women she photographed. And me.

The door closed behind the client, and I turned to face my wife.

She smiled at me, all soft curves and glowing skin, her hair twisted up in a loose knot, wisps curling around her cheeks. Her fitted pink tank top hugged the gentle curve of her swollen belly, and her black leggings made her legs look even longer.

Gemma was always fucking stunning, but there were no words to describe the perfection of my baby growing inside her.

One of her hands slid absently to her bump, rubbing the taut swell like she was checking on our little one.

I crossed the room without a word, setting my hand over hers. The movement was instinctual, as though my body couldn't be near hers without touching. I craved contact with her, no matter how small.

"You done for the day, baby?" I asked, voice low as my thumb brushed over the thin stretch of fabric that barely separated my palm from our child.

Gemma nodded, her sinful lips curving as she leaned into my chest. "Yeah. I'm excited to work with that client again, though. She said she wants to book another session after the baby's born and I'm back at work."

I grinned, tucking a piece of toffee hair behind her ear. "She's not the only one. You're booked solid for weeks. The place is buzzing, babe."

She rolled her eyes a little, but her cheeks flushed. "Quiet referrals and word of mouth have brought me more business than I ever realized they would. But you know I'm still picky. I don't shoot just anyone."

I glanced toward the back, where the reinforced steel door marked Private remained locked tight. Behind it was the vault Deviant built—secure, air-gapped, and fireproof. Nothing connected to the internet. Nothing was accessible from the outside. It was basically Gemma's own SCIF room.

"Some people think it's overkill," she murmured.

"No," I said firmly, cupping her face so our eyes were locked. "It's fucking perfect, baby. You made a fortress out of trust. You protect your clients. You're not just giving them art and a new sense of self. You're giving them safety."

Gemma's eyes softened. "They like reviewing the photos with me. I thought they'd think it was a hassle. But they say it makes them feel seen."

I lowered my head until our foreheads touched. "You have a gift, baby. Not just the camera. You see people. And you help them see themselves."

Her lips brushed mine, and she sighed dreamily. "Are we going home?"

"Yeah." I gave her a lopsided grin and tucked her into my side. "I believe I received a text that you and the baby are starving."

She gave me a mock scowl. "We are. You were supposed to feed us hours ago."

My arm tightened around her waist, and I nuzzled her temple. "Guess I better take care of you and our boy."

She melted against me, and I held her there for a long minute, breathing her in. Still couldn't believe she was mine. That I got to wake up to her tomorrow. And every day after that.

We left the studio together, one of the Iron Shield women trailing discreetly behind to lock up and reset the security system.

After what happened, I refused to let Gemma reopen the studio unless she agreed to have a guard on-site whenever she was working. She finally relented, and I'd shown her my gratitude by giving her a foot rub and several orgasms.

Female security only, though. Always. No exceptions. Not that Gemma ever asked, but I made damn sure.

The house was ten minutes away, tucked into a quiet stretch of rolling hills just past the clubhouse on the outskirts of town. We bought it the week after our wedding, which had been impulsive and perfect. One story, wide porches, and old oak trees that were perfect for swings and building tree houses. The kind of place where you could breathe, put down roots, and build something special.

We kept her cottage as well, turning one room into an office so I could work from there if she was in session. The other, we converted into a large play-room for our kids. Once the baby was born, we planned to hire a sitter to watch our little ones at the cottage while Gemma worked. That way, she could be with them between sessions.

By the time we walked into our home, the sun was dipping low, casting golden light through the wide windows and warming the honey-hued wooden floors. Gemma kicked off her sandals by the door, and I caught her hand before she could waddle toward the kitchen.

"Sit. You look tired."

She arched a brow. "I'm pregnant. I always look tired."

"Still hot as hell," I mumbled, kissing the side of her neck. "But that's not the point. Go sit down. I'm making dinner."

She laughed as I herded her toward the eating nook and gently eased her into a chair. Then I moved around the kitchen, fixing our meal while she chatted about her day and plans for tomorrow.

Once I'd grilled chicken, roasted vegetables, and

added garlic butter to the noodles, I plated everything and took it to the table. Then I went back for
two glasses of sparkling cider, her favorite.

"Dinner is served, my love."

"You're perfect," she sighed as she took her first
bite of the savory chicken.

I winked. "Only for you."

We ate slowly, talking and laughing. By the time
we finished our meal, her feet were in my lap, my
fingers rubbing small circles into her arches. She
sighed and leaned back, one hand rubbing her belly.
"If this is how you treat me when I'm pregnant, I
might just seduce you every chance I get."

"Won't hear an argument from me," I said with a
smirk.

"To being seduced?" she asked cheekily.

"Or to having lots of babies."

Gemma melted and pulled her feet down so she
could come sit on my lap. Then she kissed me
sweetly, but it quickly heated up.

I shot to my feet and carried her into our
bedroom, ignoring her weak protests as she half-
heartedly swatted my shoulder. "You're going to
throw out your back."

"Gonna throw out my sanity if I don't get you
naked in the next five minutes."

She giggled, but her breath caught when I set her down gently on the edge of the counter in our bathroom and started running water in the tub. Then I lit the candles she liked to use during her baths.

Steam curled into the air as I added her favorite oil to the water—something floral and sweet. When I turned back, she was already undressing. I joined her, stripping off my shirt, then helping her into the warm water before slipping in behind her.

Her back met my chest, and she sighed, her head lolling to one side as I gathered her hair in my fist and kissed the nape of her neck.

The water cradled us, the candlelight flickering across our damp skin. I ran my hands over the soft swell of her belly, cupped her tits, and kissed her shoulders.

She moaned, and I grasped her hips and gently lifted her, fitting the head of my cock at her entrance. Slowly, I brought her down and slipped inside her.

I gently rocked my hips up, my hands gliding up her sides and back around to fit my palms over her breasts.

"Mouth," I growled quietly.

She obediently turned her head so I could seal my lips over hers. One of my hands slipped down between her legs while the other plucked and twisted her hard nipples. When I dipped a finger between her folds, she cried out. Her pussy clenched around my shaft like a fucking vise. She started undulating, riding my cock, reaching for her pleasure.

"That's it, baby," I urged. "Ride me. Oh fuck!"

She clenched again, squeezing me so hard I nearly lost it.

I pushed her legs open wider with a palm on each thigh, then I used my index fingers to part her pussy lips and tease her center. My digits swirled around, coming close to her clit but not touching it.

"Callum," she whined, raising her arms and locking them around my neck. "Please."

"What do you want, baby?"

"Touch me," she moaned as she moved against me with more speed.

"I am touching you," I murmured with a wicked grin as I continued to tease her quivering pussy. I swiped the pad of my finger once over her clit, and she cried out as a shudder wracked her body.

"Please," she begged. "Please. I need to come."

"Then fuck me harder, baby. Ride my cock. That's it. Yes! Fuck!"

Water sloshed over the edges of the tub as we moved with more urgency, climbing toward the pinnacle of bliss. But the water was slowing us down, so I wrapped my arms around her thighs and kept her plastered against me, my shaft still buried in her heat while I pushed to my feet. Then I carefully stepped out of the tub and into our shower.

I was never more grateful for the panel I'd originally thought was ridiculous when we bought the house. In seconds, I chose a temperature and hit a button that would release the water when it reached it. The warm spray splashed onto us as I sat on the bench and moved my hands to Gemma's lush hips. Holding her in a firm grip, I moved her up and down on my shaft as I pumped up into her.

"Fucking love these hips, baby. Wide and open, so perfect for having my babies."

Gemma moaned and bounced on my cock, taking me hard and deep every time. "Callum! Oh yes! Yes!"

My palms covered her big tits, and I squeezed them as I lightly bit her neck. "Love these. Big and fat. Can't wait until they're dripping with milk. Fuck! Thinking of sucking on these leaking nipples... fuck, baby. I can't wait. Fuck! Yes! Oh fuck!"

"Yes! Callum! Harder!"

She bore down on me, and I practically saw stars. I wasn't gonna last much longer, so I pressed my finger over her clit and rubbed. Then when she was right at the edge, I pinched and sent her flying. She screamed my name, and her pussy rippled around my cock, massaging it, milking until I roared her name and exploded inside her.

Afterward, we lazily washed under the hot spray, then I took her to our bed and made slow, sweet love to her. I worshipped her body from head to toe before we climaxed together.

She curled onto her side, facing me, and draped one leg over mine, her fingers idly tracing a tattoo on my chest. For a while, we simply lay in bed, tangled in the sheets, the window cracked open to let in the night breeze.

I couldn't stop staring at the wall across from us.

There, framed in black walnut and lit by a soft sconce, was a photo of Gemma in white lace. Her body was softer now, more womanly. Hair down, cascading over one bare shoulder. She stood with her back to me, my arms wrapped around her body like a shield. One hand on her hip. The other cupping her breast. Her smile was pure mischief. Mine was hunger.

Even in stillness, the image pulsed with emotion. With my claim.

She looked up at me, then her eyes followed my gaze.

"You like it?" she asked sleepily, her mouth curved into a happy smile.

She surprised me with the photo for my birthday. I hadn't even realized she'd set the whole thing up for the picture until I opened the wrapping paper to find the beautifully framed memory.

I nodded, voice rough. "Yeah. I like it."

"It's my favorite, too."

"I look at it," I whispered, brushing her hair off her cheek, "and see everything I'll ever need."

Gemma leaned forward and pressed her lips to mine. "You're everything I never dared to want."

I kissed her deeper, pulling her close again.

And with her belly snug between us, our hearts beating in perfect rhythm, I whispered against her skin, "Forever, baby. You're mine. Forever."

EPILOGUE
GEMMA

The late afternoon sun slanted through the tall windows of my studio, casting golden light over the hardwood floors. The scent of lavender cleaner still lingered faintly in the air from this morning's tidy-up, and soft jazz played from a speaker in the corner.

I didn't have any clients today. It was just me and my favorite little assistant who never really helped. Her and the crayons she'd managed to smuggle in from the house.

"Gwinnie," I called gently. "Please remember that the walls are for looking, not coloring."

Our daughter didn't even flinch. She sat cross-legged in front of my desk, surrounded by scattered pinks and purples, her curls bouncing as she turned to grin at me. "Daddy lets me color wherever I want at his office."

"I'm sure he does," I muttered, shaking my head.

Our children had their daddy wrapped firmly around their little fingers, and his boss wasn't much better about enforcing rules when it came to the kids. His or ours.

"Not the wall, Mama," she said proudly, holding something up.

My stomach flipped when I saw what she'd been drawing on.

"Where did you get that?" I asked, racing over.

She blinked up at me, holding the photo in both hands like it was a treasure. And in a way, it was. The black-and-white print showed a younger version of me in lace lingerie and soft lighting. It was the only surviving copy from the archive that was stolen all those years ago.

It had been tucked away in the back drawer of my desk, hidden from prying eyes because my husband would have a fit if anyone else saw it. The one of us together in our bedroom was on the wall because his larger body shielded me, and that was our private space.

"Mama?" she asked again, her voice smaller this time. "Is this you?"

I crouched beside her and gently plucked the photo from her fingers. "Yes, baby. That's me."

"Were you sad?"

"No," I said softly, brushing my fingers over the edge. "I was scared...but brave, too. I didn't know it yet, but that picture helped me find something really important."

"Daddy?" she asked with a toothy grin.

I smiled. "Good guess, sweetie."

"You look pretty." She leaned her head against my arm. "It should be on the wall, too."

I kissed the top of her curls. "Daddy gets growly when people see me like that."

"Like the noise he made when Mr. Marcus said you looked pretty in your new dress?" she asked innocently. "He sounded like a doggie."

I nearly choked on a laugh. "Yes. Exactly like that."

My office door creaked open, and that growl in question echoed across the space.

"She better not be touching that damn photo," Callum muttered as he stepped in, our son right behind him.

"Too late," I called sweetly.

Corey rolled his eyes. "You can't say damn around Gwinnie, Dad."

I barely bit back my laugh at him chiding his father over his language. He took his role as big brother very seriously.

Shaking my head, I slid the photo back into the drawer where it belonged.

Callum's scowl softened when he saw Gwinnie beaming up at him.

"Hey, sunshine," he murmured, scooping her up with ease.

"I found Mama's secret picture," she announced, proud as anything.

Callum shot me a look. "We talked about locking that drawer."

"I thought I had," I muttered, aiming a smile at Gwinnie. "Apparently, our daughter is smarter than both of us."

"And me too," Corey added, patting his sister on her head with a grin.

Callum sighed, pressing a kiss to the top of her head before giving me one on my lips. "You're lucky I love you."

"Nuh-uh." Corey shook his head. "You always say you're the lucky one."

"That I do, kiddo." Callum arched a brow at our son. "But maybe you could cut your dad some slack."

Corey narrowed his eyes. "Maybe I'd do that if I had a dirt bike."

Callum jerked his thumb in my direction. "You gotta get your mom on board with that plan. Not me."

Our son turned pleading eyes toward me, and I ruffled his hair as I noticed that he'd grown another half an inch. "I suppose I can think about it."

"I ride too," Gwinnie shrieked, clapping her hands.

Callum and Corey stared at her with wide eyes, probably trying to figure out how they'd keep her off a dirt bike when she had an uncanny ability to get into just about everything.

My little angel had just bought me more time and earned herself a special treat.

Wrecker is the next Iron Rogue to claim his woman!

And if you join our newsletter, you'll get a FREE copy of The Virgin's Guardian, which was banned on Amazon.

ABOUT THE AUTHOR

The writing duo of Elle Christensen and Rochelle Paige team up under the Fiona Davenport pen name to bring you sexy, insta-love stories filled with alpha males. If you want a quick & dirty read with a guaranteed happily ever after, then give Fiona Davenport a try!

Printed in Dunstable, United Kingdom